# THE
# Connecticut
# Countess

# THE Connecticut Countess

chronicles
of Davey Bryant

## David Watmough

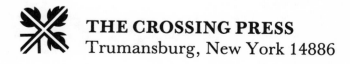

**THE CROSSING PRESS**
Trumansburg, New York 14886

Other Publications by David Watmough

Books:
*A Church Renascent* (non fiction), S.P.C.K., London, 1951.
*Names For The Numbered Years,* (Collected plays) Bau-Xi Press, Vancouver, 1967.
*Ashes For Easter* (stories) Talonbooks, Vancouver, 1972.
*Love & The Waiting Game,* (stories) Oberon Press, Ottawa, 1975, Dennis Dobson Ltd. London, 1977.
*A Cornish Landscape* (stories) Lodenek Press, Cornwall, 1975.
*No More Into The Garden* (novel) Doubleday, New York, 1978.

Anthologies:
*Stage One: A Canadian Scenebook,* Van Nostrand, Reinhold, Toronto, 1974.
*Cornish Short Stories,* Penguin Books, London, 1976.
*On The Line,* Crossing Press, N.Y., 1981.
*83: Best Canadian Stories,* Oberon Press, Ottawa, 1983.
*British Columbia/A Celebration,* Hurtig, Edmonton, 1983.

© 1984 David Watmough
Cover design by Charles Nasta
Text design and typesetting by Martha J. Waters

Printed in the U.S.A.


Library of Congress Cataloging in Publication Data

Watmough, David, 1932-
    The Connecticut countess.

    1. Homosexuals, Male--Fiction.    I. Title.
PR9199.3.W37C6    1984    813'.54    83-24080
ISBN 0-89594-124-4
ISBN 0-89594-125-2 (pbk.)

# Contents

# Author's Statement

*To underscore the fact that these are connected fictions and not fragments of autobiography I have been deliberately inconsistent with the naming of Davey's relatives from story to story and even of their relationship to him. So that he has siblings in one tale and not in another; his father is sometimes a farmer yet in one episode he is a sailor at sea. In the same spirit I have switched the terminology and topography of farms, villages and towns that Davey inhabits or visits throughout the course of the book.*

*It may not go unnoticed that this selection of the specifically gay chronicles of my protagonist ends on the high plateau of his middle age — with the valleys of his youth now traversed and the skyline of his ultimate years yet to be scaled. Later, perhaps, the whole view. Or does blindness, as a second youthful confusion, come again?*

David Watmough,
Vancouver,
British Columbia

# Sacred
# &
# Secular

I sat on the full sack of bran in the granary gloom, staring miserably out over the upper portion of the Dutch door at the rain splashing heavily on the fan leaves of the chestnut tree that blocked my view.

It was very quiet. In human sounds that is. There were only the slower and slower sobs surfacing in me a good half hour after I'd cried myself out. Otherwise there were the familiar animal noises: woodpigeons scratching on the slates of the roof above me, and the tweet of mice slipping between the stones of the rough-hewn wall, now that my huddled self had been motionless long enough to embolden them.

Below I heard the chink of chains falling away from the necks of tethered cows as, with milking long since finished, Edwin let them out — to squelch through the mud and slowly meander their way upfield.

I sat very still. I didn't want him to hear and clump up the slippery steps outside that door. I wondered if he had already untied the cattle in the other shed below the barn — and listened carefully to see if his heavy farm boots grated their steel blakeys across the granite of the lane.

"Roight, Blackie, you bugger! Off with 'ee then." A hand slapped a hairy flank, then calves lowed nervously and rustled straw. I pictured him climbing through the byre, disturbing those wide-eyed, cud-chewing calves, as he made his way to the back of the cowshed and the foot of the steps up which I'd run.

Boots thumped on the stone stairs. A rat I'd been too upset to previously notice, flashed along a rafter beam and into a hole in the wall. The mice vanished too. My shoulders slumped as a hand felt over the lower portion of the door and yanked back the flat bolt with a clatter.

I didn't move. I was sitting away from the entrance, nearer the shuttered window, opposite where the shadows were darkest. Maybe he'd go away. Maybe he'd not even seen me . . . No such luck.

"There you are then. Thought that was where you was to." His voice was low, unruffled. Then when was Edwin any other way? I got up. "What you want?"

"Jest wanted to see if you was up here agin, that's all. Might as well take a bit of cow cake down with me now I'm here, though." He took the battered metal bowl with the funny wooden handle that was lying on the floor, and scooped it full from the pile of processed cow pellets. He emptied it into a bucket whose rim was all dented and frayed.

"They send you here then? To find me? Is that it?"

"The boss man's supposed to be cutting hay up Trequite — if 'tidn' raining up that way. You know that. There's only your aunty in there."

"She sent you then?"

"No bugger *sent* Oi, Davey. I baint no one's bloody messenger boy, you do know that." He started filling another bucket, as dilapidated as the first. "Give this lot to the pigs, I will. Wish she'd boil up they kitchen scraps afore June-month is out, though. This stuff costs too much, you!"

"I don't care if you bankrupt the bugger — that's too good for 'un if you ask me!"

"He's your uncle — but *my* boss. Can't say I want to see 'un broke, you!"

I crossed the granary and watched Edwin take the bristle broom that had been leaning against the wall, and start to sweep the cow cake back into a neat pile.

"He shouted and hollered at me again this morning at

breakfast. I tell you, Edwin, if he raises his fist to me I shall call Constable Trethew down from the village."

Edwin laughed quietly. "He id'n likely to do that now, is he?"

"Why not? He've hit Jan enough times."

"That's different. That's his son, you."

"Well, he nearly hit I this morning. Would've done, I reckon, if me aunty hadn't been there. Just because I said I was going down to Wadebridge on the bus for the shopping, and not on that stupid old bike."

"He was probably gettin' at the Missus. That's the way they do usually do on it, Boy. 'Twere for her you was going down 'Bridge, wasn't it?"

"It were for him, too. For the accumulator batteries." I kicked a lumpy bag of cornmeal. "Well, I haven't gone at all — so none of 'em will be listening to the radio next week."

Edwin stopped sweeping and looked at me. "Don't make things too hard for yoursel'n, Davey."

"How'd you mean?"

He scratched his balls and gazed out at the driving rain. "Well, what with your father and mother bein' upcountry — "

"They'll be back," I shot at him.

Edwin nodded slowly at that. "I know."

Edwin was my friend. Apart from Cousin Jan, I suppose my only friend. But the way he said that "I know" irked me terribly. *What* did he know? What did *I* know? What did *any* of us know about when my father and mother would come back? Not even my uncle and aunt knew that or surely they would have told me. God knows, I asked often enough!

"What's my mother doing then? You know so bloody much!" (Why did Edwin have to look — well, so *crumpled* — when I went at him?)

"Oi didn't say I knowed it all, Davey. It's only that sitting there at the table, at mealtimes like — "

"You eavesdrop? You listen to everything?"

He tried a smile that didn't quite work. " 'Twould be hard *not* to hear with all on 'ee shoutin' at the tops of your voices."

I hated myself but I had to hurt him or something in me would have burst. "Did — did you know," I began, "that if my

*11*

aunt had had her way, you wouldn't be sitting there with us? She wanted you to take your meals alone in the linney. Said how it wasn't right for the farm boy to be eating with the boss man."

But he only looked at me with those cool gray eyes of his and shrugged immense shoulders. " 'Twould maike no difference. I don' moind me own company. Never have."

"But Uncle Ivor said to wait," I persisted. "To see if you gossiped round the village. If we didn' hear nothing back then you was to eat with the family."

That got him! Just as my instinct to hurt had told me it would. He turned and faced me fully.

"Davey Bryant, I baint never gossiped 'bout anything I did hear up 'ere to Pol'garrow. An' anyone who do say otherwise is a fuckin' liar!"

An indignation nudged his voice that I had rarely heard before. At once I felt better. More relaxed.

"All right, all right. Keep your hair on! No one said you did. I was only telling you something, that's all."

Edwin went on — only it was more to himself. "They even give up asking me questions down to the council houses. They know they won't get bugger all from me 'bout what do go on up here."

"You still haven't answered me," I said, looking out at the steady downpour alongside him. "What *is* my mother doing?"

"I — I heard as how she were driving an ambulance or somethin' up to London. Idn' that it? I dunno why you'm askin' me. You do know better than Oi."

I tried to sound unconcerned. "Oh, I don't know. Sometimes I hear things from them. Like driving an ambulance was what I heard, too. But she's never actually said so."

"Not in a letter?"

"She never writes me."

"I suspect her's bravun busy, you," Edwin muttered.

"When I was very small and my Dad was away he used to write to us, Mother and I that is, every week. Never failed."

"Well, he's got plenty on his hands, 'asn't 'er? There's a war on, Davey, don't forget that. Can't allus write when you'm at sea."

I rubbed a raindrop flat along the edge of the Dutch door; spread its wet with great care amid the crevices of blistered paint. "He doesn't even write her much either. She told me that last year when I saw her."

Edwin didn't answer right away. "I'm goin' up to Bullen to fix the hedge where the cows is breakin' through. Want to help Oi?"

"Maybe I'll come up later, Edwin. Where's Jan to? Maybe I'll come up with him and help you."

"He's taking a shit — down the orchard. Least 'ee were when I was lettin' they cows out the lower cowshouse."

"Then he should be through by now."

"Depends on what he's reading, don't it? He had *The Farmer & Stockbreeder* wid 'un, it looked to me."

"He only reads the veterinary stuff in there."

Edwin nudged me as he pulled the door open, about to brave the rain. "Well, he b'aint so bad as you wi' all they novels and that. Loike your uncle do say, Davey, you'd be there in the privy til you was faint from hunger and fall'd in, if someone didn't holler for 'ee from toime to toime!"

Edwin would've liked me to laugh, at least to chuckle. But I couldn't. On that gray and rainy morning it just wasn't in me. "Don't catch pneumonia and die," is what I said. "I don't think I could stand it if you were to go, too."

He turned on the huge square slab of slate at the top of the flight of steps. "That remoinds me," he said, "I'll take one o' they sacks for me shoulders. That were what I come up here for in the first place."

Taking one of the sacks off the dusty pile of empties, he plunged his penknife blade through the two top corners, and then threaded the rents with orange binder cord from the bale hanging on the rusty wall spike. Then he draped the sack across his shoulders and, pulling the string ends tight, made a little bow in my direction.

"Little Red Riding Hood," I said.

"Little White Riding Hood more like," he countered. And was off then into the sheeting rain. He forgot the two buckets of cow cake.

I watched him run across the muddy patch below the

granary to the semi-shelter of the fringe trees in the old orchard. My heart felt heavier than ever; my spirits so low I had to yawn and sigh to breathe properly.

When quite certain that Edwin was out of sight I shut both portions of the door. I stood in considerable gloom as the tiny window in one wall was smothered with cobwebs and dirt and scarcely catered to light at all. Opposite the Dutch doors I'd just pulled closed were those doors where I'd been sitting earlier — from which feed or straw could be tossed down to the compound below. I returned there and pushed them fully open. No one could possibly get up from the ground that way. Besides, I needed a little light.

Next I crossed to a stack of full meal bags and perched on top of them. With an almost instinctive glance around me to ensure I was alone, I slid my hand into my trouser pocket and began to play tentatively with myself. In the past year or so, whenever I felt depressed, defeated, or merely defiant, I fled to the safe sexuality between my legs for comfort.

At first nothing happened, but as I sat there in the quiet twilight I began to stir, my penis to stiffen. I lifted my fingers from my trousers to my nose and sniffed. There was the warm, animal smell of genitals — itself an excitement.

I undid my buttons and took it out. In the faint light it lay like a large white worm against the gray worsted of my pants. First it lay flaccid, to one side, but even as I stared at it, it twisted, throbbed and began to lift.

I thought of a magazine tucked away in my suitcase under the bed, over in the farmhouse. Called *Health & Efficiency* it was a nudist publication, purchased on Truro railway station on the way back to school the previous term. Just inside the cover was a woman, heavy breasted, and with a smooth, curving, belly visible before the picture hazed away in darkness at what might, or might not, have been pubic hair. I concentrated on the hope that it was as I began to rub myself slowly, backwards and forwards . . .

I must get that magazine out, I decided. Hide it over there in the granary where this jacking off business was safest. In the house, whilst reading a book at the big, polished table in the front kitchen, my attention had been nailed one night by my aunt who was seemingly talking to herself as she pushed her wooden mushroom into the heel of yet another sock and rummaged around for a wool thread in her darning basket.

"The ways you boys go through socks," she'd grumbled. "Goodness knows what you do with them — anymore than I can explain your dirty sheets up there, *except by filthy habits.*"

I had stared unseeing at the page of print before me. Her remarks may have been primarily intended for Cousin Jan who was sitting there next to me, flicking idly through the pages of *The Cornish Guardian.* But I couldn't be sure — especially as I was coming in bed each night, immediately after I had said my prayers. And often again in the mornings when I awoke to a pulsing erection and half an hour or so before my aunt screamed out that it was time to get up.

I squeezed myself more firmly, opening my legs as wide as they could go and coupling my dangling scrotum with my free hand. I had no wish to think of my aunt at that febrile moment — or of anything alien to the pleasure I was giving myself.

From the girl in the nudist magazine my succession of erotic images abruptly switched to an advertisement in a periodical I had been regularly purchasing with my pocket-money since I was twelve. This was called *Animal & Zoo* — but it was no kind of bestiality which fed my carnal make-believe. Although each issue was devoted to mammals, amphibians, reptiles and birds, news of zoos and uncommon pets, its advertisements were obviously linked to a youthful readershp, especially of boys. For every month there appeared on one of its pages a picture of a strapping youth in nothing but his underwear. An ad for shorts; it had long seemed to me as I poured over it, that the underpants displayed concealed an appendage I would dearly have liked to scrutinize and examine — for instance, in the privacy and quiet of that granary where I now played with myself.

I tore my underpants wholly free from my private parts, spitting on the palm of my hand for extra lubrication as I made to stand up and let my trousers fall to my ankles as I prepared to surrender to the last paroxysms prior to ejaculation. The movement, however, after the fairly silent activity, disturbed the other life in the granary with me. In the dark I couldn't see it, but by the weight I knew a rat had leaped from a rafter, landed on my shoe and slithered speedily across the floorboards.

Instead of the scream I intended, a weird gulp came up from my throat. Suddenly terrified that some furry malevolence down there in the crepuscular shadows of the floor would leap up my leg to clutch at my crotch, I shuddered into action. Tugging frantically at my undershorts, pushing my still hard cock back inside the 'V', even though it was painful, I then clawed at my trousers and pulled them high too.

I was still tucking my shirt in as I scurried across to the Dutch door and let myself out into the driving rain. The dark, the choking sense of grain dust and the underlying pong of the rodents who lived off it all, suddenly became a prison behind me. I bounded down the glistening steps to the ground and, once there, had to make some last minute adjustments to my clothes and slowly softening member, for comfort's sake, before slipping from outbuilding to outbuilding on my way to the farmhouse kitchen.

By the time I was peeking in at the thin figure of my aunt bent low over the kitchen range, the tumescence had gone; the sex thing thrust from my consciousness to await a more congenial time and place.

"Got a yeast bun to eat?" I called. "I'm starving."

She turned hastily from the stove. "You scared the life out of me," she said. "Yeast bun? Why, you've just had breakfast! Eat us out of house and home, you boys will, afore you'm through."

I slipped inside, put my head to the roller towel on the wall, and gave my rain-soaked hair a rub. "Where's Jan?" I asked, when the job was done.

"You tell me! Lazy young devil! You know I asked that boy to get some wood for the fire?"

"I'll get it."

"Don't bother yoursel'n. Already got 'un. Waiting for you two, I'd be here until Domesday. Here — take it then. It's burning me hand."

She handed me the piping hot yeast bun she'd just taken

from the oven. It smelled delicious. Tasted so, too. I didn't want to talk as I ate the bun in three huge, mouth-filling bites.

"I s'pose your uncle went over to Trequite to help Fred Trewin out with the hay? Never did tell Oi, one way or the other!"

"Dunno."

"An' that Jan's gone off as usual — gettin out of the work. The boy'll come to no good, I don't moind tellin' of 'ee!"

"Nope."

"Did I hear Edwin out there? Lettin' the cows out? I don't even know whether he'll be in midday or no. I tell you, Davey, here Oi am workin' and slavin' an' not knowing who's gin be home for what meal. Tid'n roight, you know, 'tidn' roight."

"No, Aunt. 'Tidn' roight."

"What you hangin' 'bout here for, then? Thought you was going into 'Bridge for me?"

"I am. Later."

"Things put off, don't get done," she admonished. But let it go at that. Then she opened the oven door again and I could see both yeast and saffron buns baking there — and on a lower shelf, rows of splits and more buns. She switched the trays around with her big oven glove, then, slamming the iron door shut, she turned her attention to the top of the stove where she had several enamel bowls of cream, scalding gently under layers of newspaper. Just the thought of that thick yellow crust forming on the clotted cream was enough to make my mouth water.

"It's illegal to make Cornish cream in wartime, did you know that?"

"Never put you off eatin' of it, has it? Anyways, you got it all wrong as usual, Davey. That's to do with a sellin' of it — not a maikin' of it."

She was wrong but I didn't want to contradict her just then. Beyond the permanent nag to her voice, the instinctive hostility to anyone speaking to her, was a slight softness, a weariness maybe, that was only rarely present. I decided to take advantage of it, feeling the need for something gentler, more intimate, than our usual exchanges. "Aunt Liz?"

"What is it now?"

I was right. There *was* a lack of hard edge to her voice. It spoke more of defeat. It encouraged me. "You know — I'm grateful for being here and that. You taking me in for the holidays each time?"

"Don't talk nonsense! If I couldn't do that for my own brother's son, what kind of person would Oi be? I ask you!"

She moved back from the oven's heat, wiped tired gray hair away from a sweat shining forehead. "I tell you, Davey, so long as you behave and don't get up to any *filth* it's a pleasure to have you. I've told you afore — this plaice is your home. It's jest as much your's as Jan's."

I knew somehow that what I was going to say next would be ill-received. But I couldn't help it. I just had to mention my mother. It was as if — well, as if just the mention of her made her more alive, more warm and real for me. "When do you think Mother will come for me?"

"I don't doubt as you'll know that afore me."

She didn't have to turn her head for me to guess her thin lips had slammed into a hard line. But I couldn't give up. Even that kind of one-way talk was better than nothing. "I know she's busy with her ambulance driving and that but — maybe she's written, Aunty, and the letter got burned by incendaries or something. Those tip-and-run raids? That's what the Jerries do, you know. Blow up a train and then skip off. And often they've caught a mail coach tacked on the back."

"Here, help me wash up these kitchen things. You can dry." She started taking pans, flour sifter, rolling pin, measuring cups, over to the sink. "Go and bring me a fresh packet of soapflakes in from the linney, there's a good boy. There's one by the copper."

I found it all right, but paused before going inside again. She wasn't going to put me off, the silly old bitch! If I wanted to talk about my mother, then we would. What did she think I was, anyway? Some little kid you only had to mention something different to, to get him off on another tack? I handed her the soapflake packet and moved over by the draining board. "Do you think Mummy and Daddy are having a bit of trouble,

Aunt Liz? You know, like with their marriage? That could be why they don't write to me any more."

There was a heavy silence. "Put that pinafore on before you start drying. I don't wash those shirts for the fun of it, you know."

I did as I was told, carefully tying the loop at the back. But I wasn't giving up *that* easily. "You haven't answered my question."

The suds in the enamel washing up bowl were agitated for the third or fourth time. "I don't know what the devil you're talking about, Davey, really I don't. How you get this nonsense in your mind beats me. Sometimes I think there's something quite unhealthy there."

"I'm not a child. I can think for myself." (I'd never dared anything like this with her before.)

"Here, dry these first. Otherwise they rust. You know I like the cutlery out the way."

Again I was careful to do as she said, waited until I was rubbing the blades of those kitchen knives as if they were sterling silver. "Even if the war hadn't happened," I persisted, "things weren't going too easy, were they?"

She sighed profoundly, her red hands suddenly stilled in the washing up water. "What on earth do you mean by that?"

"Their marriage. Mummy and Daddy. After all, they sent me down here for over three months, didn't they? And there were no bombs then."

"There moight have been. Who knew when 'twas g'in rain down bombs?"

"I'm talking about before war was declared."

"You're talking through your hat! You was only a baby. Really, you don't know *what* you'm talking about."

"You don't have to be old to know things just aren't right."

"Your father was under great strain in those days. You've no idea what the slump was like. You weren't even born!"

Her scorn was like corrosive acid. "I'm talking about when I WAS born. When my eyes had opened — and my ears. Even my dear little feathers had started sprouting."

She turned abruptly. "Are you being rude?"

I looked at myself in the dull reflection of the bottom of a saucepan. "Of course not. Just remembering . . . . Looking back, that's all."

"A kid like you! You can have no idea what it's like for your father. I often think of him — what ever you do believe, my lad. We were very close as youngsters. Did everything together we did. Jest as close as you and Jan. More so I reckon. Imagine what it must be like out there on the sea. Those corvettes or whatever they do call 'em. They b'aint very big, you. Jest think of being tossed about like a cork in one of they."

"Never knowing when a torpedo might be sliding in your direction," I said.

"Or airplanes. Or anything. And wi' your clothes sodden half the time. And your blankets. An' probably your food sopping in salt water. Terrible, Davey. Terrible . . . No, you musn't blame that one for not writing, my boy. That brother of mine got his hands full enough out there on the Atlantic."

"Mother, too," I added. "She's pretty busy in the bombing, I do know that."

My aunt didn't even bother to cover up her change of tone. "For your mother it's different. Then she never were a good correspondent. Never knew when she were going to turn up here on the farm with you — until she were actually coming down the farmyard there."

"You know, Aunt Liz, I do think Mummy actually likes the air-raids. The excitement and all that."

I was standing behind her shoulder so still couldn't see her face. But I could imagine that thin old lip curling upwards, this time.

"Wouldn't put it past her. Easily bored, your mother always was. Anything for distraction — anything, that is, 'cept a bit of housework. Her never did like any of the ordinary things . . . cooking and cleaning for instance."

"Our house were always clean," I said defensively, giving a flour bowl an extra rub as I did so.

"Depends on what standards you do have for a start, don't it? Never too busy to put her hat and coat on for a jaunt. I always remember that about your mother. A lick and a promise housekeeper, she was. Why, her used to say so herself! 'Half a minute, Liz,' she'd say when I come downstairs and offered to give her a hand. 'Half a minute and I'll be all through! Just takes a lick and a promise and I can join you for a trip into town and a spot of shopping.' Then she didn't believe in polishing behind things. 'What the eyes don't see, the heart don't grieve over, Lizzy' — that were something else she used to say, too."

"I know she didn't believe in making too much fuss about stupid little things," I said murderously. "Like the Hoover could vacuum on its own without her having to pick up and bang her carpets every five minutes."

I watched her neck, hoping it would flush. That was a direct attack. Not a day went by when Aunt Liz wasn't out there at the clothesline in the mowey, banging away at her carpets with her frayed beater. I got a loud sniff in return. "Well, it takes all sorts to make a world I s'pose. It's just that your mother wasn't really the domestic sort, that's all."

Two things happened next, more or less simultaneously. I popped the question I'd been dying for ages to ask her. "You don't really like my mother, do you Aunt Liz?" And at the same time, as I reached forward to pick up the heavy cast-iron frying pan to wipe dry, I farted. Nothing noisy. Silent rather, and very long. I couldn't help it. It just slid out. In half a tick I could smell it. It was a real ponger. I bit my lip in embarrassment.

She didn't answer my question right away. Then she started, slowly picking up speed. "Of course I'm fond of your mother. That wasn't a very nice thing to say, Davey. I've never made any distinction between you and Jan — and there's none can say I have. I don't think you'm always fair to me —" She broke off. I could guess what was coming. It wasn't very difficult with that stink of mine filling the hot little kitchen. "Davey? Did you . . . Have you just been filthy? . . . Did you make —?"

"I broke wind," I said, the suspense driving me mad. "I'm sorry but it just came out. I —"

"Stop it!" she shouted. "I don't want to hear! You're nothing but a dirty little beast. Now get out! Get outside and stay with those animals out there. You'm jest loike 'em. Go on!"

It wasn't just the embarrassment — though that was real enough. My face burned. You just didn't fart in front of Aunt Liz. I went to the door and unlatched the upper half. I couldn't see properly out towards the haystack. My sight was blurred.

"Go on," she snapped. "Out there until 'ee can mend your manners. I don't want 'ee in my kitchen 'til you learn to behave."

"Fuck you!" I said under my breath as I pulled the bolt of the lower half and walked out of doors.

It had stopped raining. In fact the sun was breaking through and little spirals of steam were rising from the ground. I made for the lower orchard and the outdoor privy that stood just by it.

"Jan?" I called softly, when I was a few feet away from the faded green door. "Jan, you still in there?"

But there was only the tiny sound of moisture all around me as it drained into the earth. Good, I thought. I'll slip in there and finish off what I started in the granary. I sat down quickly on the cold wooden seat, then stretched my foot out as far as it would go to jam the door shut from unwanted intruders. . . .

# Seduction

A little mustached man in Berlin barked an order and I was separated for the first time in my life from my best friend. We were both fourteen and had played together, learned at school together, and done childhood chores together on our fathers' neighboring farms since we were five.

Jan's dad, who had given up farming a year before, because seemingly no-one in England wanted to buy produce raised on our Cornish farms during the Depression, was immediately called up at the outbreak of war, joined the army and was posted to a camp on the outskirts of London. In a matter of months his whole family left our village and stayed as close to him as they could manage.

On the other hand we Bryants went on as if Hitler had never happened. Oh, we listened to news broadcasts about armies dashing around Europe, with the Germans always suffering losses from our chaps but somehow always winning and taking first cities, then whole countries. And later, of course, we heard on the B.B.C. and read in the *Daily Express,* of London being bombed. But, our primary reality was those newly-ploughed fields which for years before the war had stood unkempt in shaggy weeds, knee-high sorrel, and purple thistles even taller.

I had my milk-round before going off to school each morning. And there was milking to be done after school now that our cows had increased from five to seventeen. There were other changes. First my older brother went off to join the Navy. Then, only a few months later, my other brother, Wesley, volunteered for the Royal Marines. I was now all alone.

Father let me do things that he hadn't before. I took the cows that were "looking for the bull" (you could tell because they started mounting each other's backs) over to Dunstan's farm to be mated with their gigantic Ayrshire stud. I kept my own ducks, sold eggs and birds, and carefully totted up my sales, and balanced them with expenditures in a little black book.

At Monday market in Wadebridge, when I often skipped school, grumpy old men like Mr. Pengelly who farmed Tregillers, now nodded at me as well as Dad. Why not? Hadn't I sold him some of my best Khaki Campbell ducklings a couple of weeks before? But Mr. Pengelly did more than just nod.

"You got a good head on 'ee, Boy — Oi'll tell 'ee that. You'm your father's son when it do come to sellin.' " He turned to his pipe-sucking cronies. "Boy's only got to put a bit of shit in his shoes and git some hair on his faice — an' 'er moight jest be taken for a man, you!"

Feeling the burn on my over-smooth cheeks as he and his semi-circle of friends chuckled like oafs in agreement, I fled them that particular market day for the safety and stench of the strong-smelling urinal in the courtyard of The Dolphin. I undid my fly and inserted my finger to rub myself below the navel and just above my cock.

'Well, to hell with those fuckers!' I could feel hair there all right, even make out some strands. Not much. Nothing like on the men I'd seen when standing in similar places and had peered down cautiously at those who had opened their pants more widely than was strictly necessary for just taking a piss.

I did up the buttons of my corduroy pants and in an almost involuntary gesture, let the same hand rub my chin. That depressed me all over again. I recalled my father's tired old remark — 'as smooth as a baby's bottom' which he constantly used to describe my face: not realizing, I think, how much I hated it.

I'm not just talking about being a boy, you see. What you've got to understand is that it was wartime: everyone who was anyone wore a uniform. The only goal of a boy's existence in wartime is TO GET GROWN UP.

That same week when I could have machine-gunned old Pengelly into Kingdom-Come for his stupid crack, Mother read out a letter to us as Dad and I sat down to supper in the back kitchen. "Well, it looks loike Davey is going to see his ole friend Jan again." She stuck Dad's glasses on the end of her nose — the only way she could see to read through them. She'd never felt there was enough money to have a pair of her own. "This 'ere is from Edie. They've been bombed out and Fred is g'in be off to some plaice where they can't be wid 'un."

"Overseas, Eileen. That's what *that* do mean," Dad told her.

"So we is going to take up your offer, Eileen," Mother read out in her Cornish accent, "And Jan and me will come down on the Atlantic Coast Express from Waterloo on the 18th. I have written Aunt Mathilda and she says as how we can have the cottage next to hers. But it do need a cleaning up, pretty ways, as there b'aint been anyone living there since Uncle Harry died. So if we could stay with all on you to Pentinny for a week or two, I should be grateful. Jan has applied to be — what's this word then, Father?"

"Cadet," my father supplied.

"Cadet in the Merchant Navy. But they do say he won't hear nothing for some weeks. Reckon he can go back to school in Bodmin if they'll take him. Otherwise I daresay Tom can use him on the farm — you can that, can't 'ee, Father?"

Dad nodded.

"You will hardly recognize our Jan, he has shot up so. Taller than his father, if you can believe it . . . "

I couldn't. Nor did I want to. They still called me 'little shrimp' at school. I wriggled on the wooden bench alongside the trestle table as I waited for Mother to finish reading aloud all the boring stuff that Aunt Edie (as I had called her since childhood) had to say, and mentally checked off the things I had to show Jan and to tell him. That is, the ways I hoped to impress him. But by the time Mother had finished the letter and served the pasties I still hadn't got much of a list . . .

It wasn't hard to persuade Dad to let me take the mare, Ruby, in the cart to meet the Treharrocks at St. Kew Highway station, as he was busy with the other two horses cutting a neighbor's hay over to Trequite. Mother was more difficult, though, when I said I intended wearing my new sports jacket and my best long pants — my *only* long pants, to tell the truth.

But I did anyway, conscious of the fine trouser crease achieved through inserting them between mattress and bottom sheet the night before, as I sat there impatiently flicking the horse flies off Ruby's broad rump with the slack reins as I awaited the express train from Upcountry.

It's funny the things you remember — with me, as Jan and Aunt Edie climbed down from the first of the two railway carriages, it was the sudden and savage drying of the throat as I saw a self-assured giant throw two battered old suitcases down on the platform, turn, and wave cheerily to me.

Jan? Never in your life! That — that hulking great lout my old friend? I cringed as they approached. I should have gotten down from the cart, of course, and given them a hand with their luggage. But will you believe me when I say I couldn't? What I did was freeze until they stood by the shafts of the cart. I dared not look at him. I let my eyes focus only on Aunt Edie. I jumped down and kissed her like a lover. She, after all, had not deserted me. Had not changed . . .

"Hello, Davey," he said.

It was a deep voice I'd never heard before.

"How — how are you, Jan?" It was no good. I couldn't even lower my own voice a single note.

Thank God Aunt Edie more or less took over from then to when we arrived at the farm; rattling on about nothing. We two boys just sat silent, occasionally sliding each other covert glances as we strove to sum each other up: confused by the magic changes wrought by a couple of pubescent years.

At least, I was confused. If the enormous height of my erstwhile constant companion was perplexing, and the changed voice with its infuriating assurance, a grating sound on the twilight air of early summer, that faint smudge of hair between Jan's nose and upper lip was a badge of supremacy I could hardly bear! As children together it was *I* who had always been the leader: suggesting games and escapades, picking quarrels when beset by strange moods, and always taking the initiative when reconciliation was called for. But now, as I made Ruby trot more quickly than the old cart horse was accustomed to, through the midge-and-gnat-swarming dusk, I realized with forlorn bitterness that there was to be no easy falling into familiar roles where I had invariably assumed that of boss. I tried, mind you — the very next day. I was naturally able to show him changes on the farm and as I was on home ground I felt I could keep my end up. But an enlarged dairy herd, my thriving troup of Khaki Campbell ducks, even my new ferret, Fury, elicited from him no more than a casual grunt. His lack of interest stung like vinegar on a cut finger.

Frantically I thought of other means to impress. "I must show you my bit of Junkers 88 — the Gerry that crashed in Tehiddy Meadows. I got up there before any of 'em. Got a whole wing strut. The bullets was still bursting in the heat, you! I hid the strut in my lumber jacket when Constable Trethew got up there and started to chase us away."

Jan didn't speak but suddenly lifted his leg up on one of the fallen apple trees in the old orchard we were crossing. He pulled up his trouser leg, his left one. "See that," he said in his hideous Paul Robeson voice. "I got that when our house was blitzed. I was unconscious for 24 hours."

Where he'd exposed the calf of his leg was a very thin red scar: a delicate line about three inches in length. Very impressive. But it wasn't what impressed me most. He'd pulled up his trouser higher than was necessary for his boasting. What I saw and what made my throat contract and forced me to lick lips, were the light gold curls of hair descending below his thigh and even on his shin. My legs were utterly devoid of hair and have remained so till this day. "You'm a hairy bugger!" I forced a little laugh from somewhere. "Must have gorilla blood in 'ee, Jan!"

With that he let his trouser drop back into place, leaped up on the lichen-furred trunk, turned in my direction and began to thump his chest. "Ah-ah-ah-ah-ah" — as Tarzan's cry rang out amid the ancient apple trees, a woodpigeon flapped noisily away from upper branches, and other ringdoves immediately stopped their summer cooing.

Thank God *something* from our shared past! I straightway began to shuffle-dance up and down, my arms distended loosely at my sides. "Uh-uh-uh-uh-uh" — I did my Cheetah, the chimpanzee, impersonation. Then both of us, laughing, shouting, making animal and bird calls, crashed our way through the bramble undergrowth.

As the hours passed I began to get used to Jan's new height, and even his voice ceased to shock so violently every time he opened his mouth. In fact I let myself be lulled into a false sense of security, telling myself that apart from these novelties, it was still the same old Jan under the skin.

Until, that was, we reached the edge of Poltreworgey Woods and flung ourselves down in their shade and quietly sucked the sweetness out of long grass stems. I couldn't see his expression as we both lay looking up through the twig tracery of a dead elm at an unsullied sky and a June-hot sun. And I was certainly glad he couldn't read mine when he suddenly broke the silence. "What the girls like around here, then? Got one special in mind for me, Davey?"

My mind raced like a ferret through a rabbit warren — for while this was territory that fascinated, it was one I had never entered. But I would cheerfully have stood blindfolded before a firing squad rather than tell Jan that. "Well, there's Audrey up to Pengarrow. You was always sweet on her, weren't 'ee?"

"Oh, I didn't mean some kid. One that don't mind a good old thrash 'round — you know."

(Oh, oh if only I did!) "There's Rosemary Jago at school, then. She's a handsome enough maid, I don't mind tellin' 'ee."

"Well, do she or don't she? That's the important thing."

"I can tell 'ee that there b'aint no one down Tredizzick — that's where she's from — that don't call her a bravun huzzy, if that's anything."

"You had her, then?"

Feeling my virginity like venereal disease I lied swiftly. "Only the once. Too bloody busy you! What wi' school and helpin'

Dad out — now there b'aint no one else."

"I don't want some girl what's all kiss and cuddle and then hands off. Where I come from they know what it's all about. No wasting time. Grikey! Makes me feel horny just to think about what I left behind up there. I hope these maids, Davey, can do ̣as well."

As he said 'maids' I realized that was the first real Cornish expression he'd used since he got off the train. It saved him, if he did but know it, from hearing me defend the sensuality of Cornish girls I'd never had. "You've just forgotten, Jan," I told him. "You've been away too long."

"Boy! Those London girls! You c'n have no idea, Kid. They're on their backs as soon as you look at 'em." Jan sighed. And as it was obviously at an image formed of his metropolitan sex life, I felt excluded. Worse . . . rejected.

I jumped abruptly to my feet. "Come on," I said, "I got more to show you." Actually what I did was to lead him via a circuitous route back towards the farm. It wasn't so much that I had a specific plan; rather that I had become quite incapable any longer of lying there in the grass listening to his manly exploits.

When we got home it was to find that Mother and Aunt Edie had taken the bus into Wadebridge. I lead the way in through the clock-ticking, empty house after reading Mother's note, towards the front parlour. I had a strange sense of trespass at entering the recesses of an indoor world which I was usually forbidden except on Sundays.

· "There's something you can help me with," I called over my shoulder.

"What you doing?" he asked a few minutes later as, kneeling on the thick carpet in the rarely used room off the front kitchen, I began to pull several boxes out from behind the green curtain screening the corner next to the spinet around which we sang hymns on Sabbath evenings.

"My train set. I want to put it up. Remember it?"

"You still play with *that*?" Incredulity thickened his voice.

"Not very often. Too busy, you. But I want to make sure it's in full working order before I sell it. There's a kid in school that's interested. You'll give us a hand, won't 'ee?" What else could he say when I put it like that? So he got down on the floor, too, and started putting the rails together.

"Should be doing this when it's raining," he grumbled mildly. "Better to be outside on a day like this."

I at once set out to mollify him. Somehow it was very important at that moment not to have Jan grumpy with me. "If it hadn't been your first day, Dad would never have given me the time off. Certainly not during hay-making. And I could get a couple pound for this, Jan. I've been a bit broke lately and I thought if I could make some money I could take of 'ee down to the dance in Bodmin the week after next. You'd best be saving your own pennies until you start work for Father." He didn't say thank you or anything like that — but it certainly shut him up.

As soon as we'd got a good-sized figure-eight down on the floor, replete with level-crossing, points, and passenger bridge with signal gantry over the tracks, I wound up the clockwork locomotive, hitched up the four carriages, and got it going. The engine came off the track at the points — not once but twice.

"Would 'ee moind checkin' 'em, Jan? You was always better than me with they things." I squatted very close to him as he bent over the faulty mechanism to investigate further. I noticed that his tongue peeped out just a bit between his lips as he worked. Inwardly I smiled. That at least was something of the old Jan I remembered from the past. "Here," I said, "shall I hold it while you fiddle with that?"

Being shorter than he was I was thus closer to the ground. Very carefully I edged myself under his arms so that my elbow was just an inch or two between his legs as he sat back on his haunches. With even greater care I maneuvered myself so that I could feel my shirt at the elbow, brush against his fly. Then I moved my arm gradually back so that it was no longer my elbow but my hand clutching the points that actually rested about his crotch.

"Got a pair of pliers?" His eyes didn't leave the points as he tried to bend the lever that moved them.

"Here," I said, grabbing them from the carpet with my unoccupied hand and thanking my lucky stars that I had thrown them out when emptying the cardboard boxes.

As he put pressure on the pliers I let my hand sink down more firmly on the center of his anatomy. And closed my eyes as I felt the first nudging of something stiffening there. From outside came the sound of swallows twittering about the front porch and, I think, the noon train from Padstow whistled before entering Trelill tunnel. But where we two sat on the parlor carpet was an almost palpable silence. Only the breathing of both of us was discernable as Jan worked on the railroad points, and I so subtly, so gently, worked on him . . .

"There," he said suddenly, "that's got it." And with no more excuse for its presence, I naturally had to move my hand away from his genitals. But not before letting my fingers describe the full length of his tumescence.

The atmosphere had changed though I think neither of us would have dared make reference to the fact. Jan's sexual awareness was now emphatically revealed within his pants. Emboldened, I eased my own hardness from one side of my trousers to the other. We took infinite care not to look into each other's face but by now I felt taken over by a profound sense of cunning: the kind of alertness and response an animal knows when it is hot on the scent of its quarry. When Jan stood up and spoke it was as I had actually willed the words that came out of his mouth.

"Think I'll use the lav. Back in a minute."

I stood up, too, my eyes indifferent to all save that bulge in his pants, as with a funny sort of walk (yes, he was so stiff down there that it actually affected his movement) he turned and, passing me, left the room.

I waited, stroked myself mechanically a couple of times, as I listened for the heavy creaking of the farmhouse stairs. When I heard the door of the new bathroom that Father had installed only that spring in what had been my brother Wesley's room, I acted quickly. Knowing every creak on those ancient stairs, and, correspondingly every safe plank of silence, I made my way upstairs without a sound. Outside the bathroom door I waited a few extra seconds to give him time to lower his clothes

31

and sit down. Then I knelt and peered through the keyhole, knowing before my eye could focus around the clumsy, oldfashioned lock (there was no key) what I would see.

No question of disappointment: instinct had served me well. He was sitting there, legs spread apart, playing slowly with his aroused cock. Once he looked furtively towards the door, then returned to the slow and deliberate stimulation of himself. "Jan," I called, surprising myself at the hoarseness of my voice. "Jan, I can see what you're doing."

The effect of my words reminded me of films I'd seen of a man in the electric chair. He jerked and shot up as if fifty thousand volts were passing through him. But the look on his face as the most secret, intimate, self-expression was violated, quite frightened me.

"Jan," I repeated quickly. "It doesn't matter. I feel that way, too." With that I stood up, opened the bathroom door and stepped across to him. He was half-standing, his trousers pulled frantically to somewhere above his knees. I took hold of his stiff member, speaking softly. "I'm horny, too. But not here. They may be back. Let's go over to the granary."

"I could do with a fuckin' good girl," he muttered. But I saw that was mechanical, face-saving. With a collapsed feeling inside I knew the relief of triumph. Passively, almost like a little child, he let me put it away for him; do up his buttons and lead him out of the bathroom. With him following closely I led the way determinedly to that little nest at the back of the granary where in the pathetic rhythm of short-circuited sex, I had so often toyed with my own person while thinking of kindred experiences to those that Jan had actually had. Then I forgot everything except the frantic passion of his body . . . .

It never happened again between us — though if I cling to that honesty which is so hard, I have to say it was beautiful. For me the biggest sense of physical release I had ever known in my farm-girl life. I don't just mean the seduction of Jan. I mean the fulfillment Jan gave me.

Shortly after, at least by the end of the summer, Jan had his keenest ambition realized and joined the Merchant Service as a cadet. That was where, as he so often told me, he would find at every port those girls whom he wished to 'bang into next week.'

Just before that little, mustached man collapsed in the bunker dust of Berlin's ruins, a rusty, old British freighter a hundred miles off the mouth of the river Amazon, and stuffed with explosives for the war in the Pacific, met a torpedo from a U-boat. There were no survivors but a man on another ship saw the Lanivet Castle go as high in the heavens as it finally sank in the sea. And so, over two years later, Aunt Edie learned that her Jan had passed in official records from merely "missing" to "drowned at sea." Jan was sixteen. He never did have all the girls his anxious body had wished. He died and I lived, and that is the way of it.

But I like to think that in a dusty memory, locked forever by further deaths from those it would have caused pain and embarrassment, had they ever found out, something of my friend Jan continues to live. Crude, perhaps pathetic, but while I survive, laughing and crying through life, a little of Jan is carried carefully, deep in me.

# The
# Cross-Country
# Run

In 1943 I was living in Frome, Somerset because my London
school had been evacuated there. This was not a happy time of
my life. The reasons for this were multiple but I will only give a
few.

Most important, or so I think now, years later as a fifty-year-
old man hindsighting a fifteen-year-old boy, was my home-
sickness. I missed my stepmother and I thoroughly hated this
part of Somerset precisely because it differed from the Cornwall in which I was raised and which I now only saw during
holidays. For instance, I disliked the general appearance of the
countryside because it lacked the stout, stone hedges of my
native Duchy. I loathed the very beasts of the field because the
cattle were smaller, rangier, and of different breeds from those
to which I was accustomed on our Cornish farm. The Somerset
sheep were smaller and the pigs longer. I missed the cob of
Cornish walls, despised the pretty thatch of roofs in their
sissified villages and ached for Delabole and Penpethy slate for
both tiles and building materials which so happily saved North
Cornwall from the picturesque.

And then there was school. Apart from a couple of friends I
was something of an anti-social figure. I wasn't exactly un-
popular but nor was my company much sought, even had I
wished it. This was because I was considered eccentric and the

genesis of this reputation was my quite explicit preference for the company of other than human forms of life — particularly that of mammals and birds but with a generous sprinkling of reptiles and amphibians.

Much of my free time was devoted to observing, tracking, capturing and then taming a variety of creatures — from hedgehogs and squirrels to magpies and jackdaws, with the occasional grassnake and newt as light relief as they needed less effort to secure and maintain.

But my schoolfellows simply did not share my predilections and for the most part, tolerantly ignored me. There were one or two bully-boys who made my life a misery by threatening to hurt my pets but such blemishes to the complexion of life were stoically accepted by one who inclined to even greater fatalism than most boys away at school.

There was one youth, though, who sought to persecute me on moral grounds. He often flared at me, hissing that I lacked any school spirit and that I was indifferent to the outcome of that war which raged at the circumference of our lives. The specific reason for this latter accusation involved my form's patriotic renting of an agricultural *allotment* from the Frome Town Council in order to cultivate a 'Victory Garden,' as current usage had it.

In short weeks the rich Somerset loam was rendered invisible by seas of perpetual spinach, beets, potatoes and the like. Now my own contribution to this theme of food for a U-boat blockaded nation, was the breeding of Belgian hares (rabbits) for the table. Unfortunately, my efforts at woodwork were inferior to my indubitable abilities at animal husbandry and on numerous occasions, owing to faultily nailed wire-netting and ill-fitting hutch doors, another generation of my rapidly multiplying rabbits would escape and find both shelter and sustenance among the crops of my schoolmates. It was when Ian McDermott, the super-patriot who despised my introverted attitudes to so many things he held dear, had all his carrots demolished by my errant bunnies, that he railed against my irresponsibility towards feeding the nation.

I was to recall his almost incoherent venom on a subsequent

occasion when I was in headlong conflict with another aspect of school life to which I must now refer. Organized sports were anathema to me and I was never more diligent than in my efforts to avoid involvement in them or to deceive those in authority who strove to implicate me in the kicking or hitting of balls; in running, jumping, or swimming in competition.

Of all these uncongenial activities, cross-country running was the one I abhorred most. So that one sunwashed afternoon, when I found myself incapable of dodging the suspicious eye of Mr. Hammond, our phys-ed teacher, I determined that I would duck out of his stupid race just as soon as it proved practical and I stood a fair chance of returning later, undetected by the oaf who had planned the event.

My specific detestation of this cross-country business involved the fact that it took place across the very terrain which I cherished as a naturalist's kingdom. Along the selfsame tracks which were shortly to see a score or more of yelling, panting boys in their muddied white singlets and shorts, I could have been found on almost any weekend, dressed quietly to camouflage my presence, and walking slowly enough to sniff the air for animal scents and to ensure at the same time that I cracked no twigs, brushed no foliage, to give myself away.

I knew I could not forsake their tiresome company until we reached the edge of the woods near Nunny Ketch. But I was able, owing to my intimate familiarity with that countryside, to anticipate the very tree up which I would shin to hide from the others and, more importantly, from Mr. Hammond himself. Imagine my frustration, then, when after gently slowing to the rear of the pack, I found myself in consort with the exigent Ian McDermott who, if he saw me in the act of abandoning the cross-country run, while being too morally upright to rat on me, would certainly take out his righteous wrath upon my body. The choice between a battering from him and a caning from the hairy hand of Mr. Hammond was of no great moment to me. I did not like physical hurt from whatever quarter!

The situation was growing desperate when I gasped to McDermott that my shoelace was becoming loose, and slackened speed even more palpably. I could have throttled him when he slowed down, too.

Salvation came from on high. Just as I drew to a halt and he inclined likewise, there came a high-pitched whine of engines in the cloudless heavens. Shielding my eyes from the sun's glare with my cupped hand I was able to see the silver specks of airplanes miles up. And realized from the spasmodic chatter of machine guns that a dogfight between our fighters and Jerry was taking place up there.

We had already enjoyed two previous daylight raids on the Fulton aircraft works in nearby Bristol and were thus conversant with such airborne excitement.

"Better scatter," I yelled to McDermott. "Remember when those Jerries strafed the cricket field? And we're wearing white again today."

"We must keep together, Bryant. There's safety in numbers."

He said something else but I didn't hear as I had already dived into the concealment of the forest. My last impression of him, though, was of a face full of doubt — disbelieving my action had any connection with the aerial battle overhead. For a while there, I was unable to put McDermott's countenance out of my mind. No one likes to receive such an intense expression of mistrust — certainly not me.

But there was work to do and an ancillary opportunity to suppress uncomfortable images. On reaching the tree I had first to jump up and catch the bough of the elm I had selected before climbing higher and higher through its branches. When I finally paused for breath I could still hear boys shouting as they crashed through the bushes. But I assumed it was as cheering supporters for the spitfires or hurricanes overhead and not related to my defection.

I found myself a comfortable crevice between two main boughs and settled to wait. I knew the route old Hammond would take and, if I estimated correctly, I would be able to double back on my tracks and join them, my absence undetected, before we returned to the school grounds and the signing-off register.

In the past I had found this particular tree useful for observing badgers at dusk, on their way to a stream. You had to have a comfortable place and one preferably above ground. That way you were less likely to shift your body and make a noise — which would have sent them scampering back to the sett. And it was also a precaution up there against their lifting moist black muzzles and catching your scent which would have also rapidly brought about their disappearance.

I must have been there half an hour or so when I heard a noise. Indeed, I first thought it was one of the badgers making an uncharacteristic, diurnal expedition through the woods. But as I listened harder and strained to peer down through the screen of leaves, I concluded that the intermittent sounds were in fact distinctly unbadger-like. They were more cautious, and had too long pauses between each to persuade me they belonged to my stripe-headed friends.

Then I saw the man crouched down there, almost right beneath me. It was an airman. But the uniform he was wearing was not that of the R.A.F. I realized with choking excitement that I was looking at a German. A member, I decided, of the *Luftwaffe*. He had blond hair. Very blond, almost white. I told myself that he was one of Hitler's aryans that I had read about. I remembered they were against the Jews, these people, and that made me recall Charlie Lazarus, one of my two best friends at school.

From my hopefully invisible vantage point I studied the Jerry airman. He was quite young; could have passed for a school prefect, come to that. Apart from the straw colored hair he had a rather nice pug face which vaguely reminded me of Gibson, the captain of our School House, who had joined up in the airforce the year before and was now undergoing training somewhere in Canada, they said.

The uniform looked odd, but I suppose that was just because I was so used to what our own looked like by seeing them every day. And this was one I had never set eyes on before. Our aircraft recognition books showed us every kind of Jerry plane but not the uniforms of the people that flew in them.

My survey didn't linger very long over such sartorial matters. I could see a dark stain about the top of his arm and guessed he was wounded. As he crouched there his right hand went up and clasped the opposite shoulder, and over his fingers ran bright streams of blood. That fascinated me more than anything else. I wondered if he was dying. I thought of myself later, telling Charlie Lazarus and Dennis James that I had watched a dying Jerry in the woods near Nunney Ketch. They probably wouldn't believe me. Then I had the daft notion that I really needed a bit of his uniform — a badge or something — as a souvenir. They would *have* to believe me then . . .

He moved his position from amid the heap of ferns where I had first spied him. He had pitched forward now by the trunk of my tree and was actually kneeling. I thought of school chapel and wondered if Germans like him ever said their prayers.

A strange thing happened. I swear I didn't move, didn't make a sound. But suddenly we were looking at each other, eye to eye.

"Hello," he said. "You up there."

I didn't answer. I was not afraid, exactly, but I dearly wished he had not looked up and seen me through my screen of elm leaves.

He spoke again. "What is your name? Mine is Gerhard."

So friendly! My mind was racing. I could so easily hate his uniform: that was The Enemy. He was quite another matter. I wished he hadn't told me his name.

"Ich bien ein englisches Knabe," I informed him. "Sie sind Deutsch, nein?" (I knew a moment of self-reproach at my inattention during Herr Gottlieb's boring German class.) But I need not have worried. This Gerhard insisted on speaking in English. Perhaps he thought it the polite thing to do, having just landed in England uninvited, from the skies, as it were.

It occurred to me that perhaps he was a spy — with all that good English at his command. One more reason not to clamber down the elm tree, which was what he was now suggesting. I just sat there staring silently at him as he persisted in his entreaties.

"I am hurting. If you would please come down the *Baum*. Tree, I am sorry. Sometimes I forget English. I have been from the Gymnasium so long. But I cannot get my hand to where it bleeds, see?" He made a gesture and I understood all right.

I thought just one question to him might be in order. "You do that when you crashed?" I called down.

"My parachute gets caught up there in a tree. I fall all the way to the ground. I have bullet wound too. I am quite sick. If you would help me, please?"

Slowly I relented. His face had become whiter since we had first looked at each other and I was convinced that dark stain about his uniform had grown. It would do no harm if I went down a few more branches, the better to inspect him. I descended to a point where I estimated he still could not jump up and grab me. From this position I could examine him more comprehensively.

There were several objects about his person, including his goggles and a pair of super leather gauntlets, which I would have dearly loved as souvenirs. I started, guiltily, at my lack of humanity when he was obviously suffering. One of his boots had been torn off and I now noticed that his forehead was scratched and his uniform considerably muddied.

"You look a bit of a mess," I called down. "What you need is a doctor. But when you surrender as a prisoner-of-war, you'll get all that."

"I am losing blood. Will you help me now? I shall soon lose the consciousness."

Not quite sure what to expect, I shrugged, got up, and climbed down to the bough from which I could safely swing to the ground, and then jumped.

"Do you have a revolver?" I asked nervously, once more on *terra firma* but keeping my distance.

"I lost it coming through the trees when the parachute harness broke. But why you worry about a gun? *Gut Gott,* I am not going to hurt you!"

I was somewhat mollified. "What you want me to do?"

He explained that he wanted me to take his outer garments off to get to his undershirt. That, he explained, could be used to staunch the bleeding, at least temporarily. And he also asked me to wipe his face which at close quarters, I could now see, was beaded in sweat.

I did all these things he requested. As I worked I had a weird sense of contentment. I *liked* looking after my German airman and, contrary to my expectations, (based on the experience of being punched on the nose during a playground altercation) didn't even feel faint this time at the sight of blood. I noticed that he smelled differently from us. I supposed it was because he used German soap. He did not use Brylcream or anything on his hair so the odd, cheesey smell had nothing to do with hair-dressing.

As I worked on his face, noticing that his eyes were blue and that there were tiny little hairs along the ridges of his cheeks, I suddenly felt embarrassed by our intimacy.

"We hate Hitler over here," I announced abruptly. "And at school we got lots of Jews including Charlie Lazarus my best friend." But he didn't reply. Merely closed his blue eyes and kept clenching and unclenching his hands.

I tried again. "We hate Nazis, you know."

He re-opened his eyes. "What do you do here in the forest?" he asked.

I was at once suspicious again. "Badger watching," I announced, suppressing cross-country running.

He looked puzzled. "Badger?"

With all the enthusiasm a naturalist can muster, I embarked upon a description. But I had not gone much beyond the striped head and squat, silver-gray body when he actually laughed with recognition. "Ein Dachs!" he exclaimed. "Ein Dachs!"

It was my turn to comprehend. "Dachs — dachshund," I said. "Of course. My dog book says dachshunds are used for badger hunting in Germany."

Somehow our relationship was different from that moment on. Try as I might, I couldn't see this Gerhard as our national foe. He told me that he, too, had gone badger-watching in the woodlands of the Hartz Mountains, his homeland. As I bathed his face — by now somewhat unnecessarily — I felt that he was more an ally than enemy. Certainly I seemed closer to him than to most of those at my school.

"What else interests you, Daffey, after the badgers?" I had revealed my name, as you can see, and was about to reveal a whole lot else.

"I like all animals," I told him readily. "And might be a vet after the war. But I don't like organized games which is why you found me up that tree. I'm a Cornishman," I added, "and I don't like it here in Somerset half as much."

He took time to digest all that, closing his eyes again. "Cornwall — that is *Tristan Und Isolde*. Our Wagner wrote his opera on the King of Cornwall. King Mark?"

"Did he?" I replied, not knowing too much about Tristan and Isolde and nothing whatever about the opera.

"We got King Arthur and Merlin's Cave at Tintagel. And Sir Launcelot and the sword Excalibur at Dozemary Pool."

"You love this Cornwall, Daffey, I can see that is so."

I couldn't help it. My eyes misted. "It is the nicest place in the world for me," I told him, "though I don't always get on as well with my Dad as I ought to."

There was a small silence between us, after which Gerhard sat up a little, pushing the torn garments I had fashioned into crude bandages, against his shoulder.

"I too, Daffey, have my Hartz mountains. That is why I am in this uniform and in your country. Perhaps it is that all of us who love too much our special place are doomed."

"I don't know what you mean," I said carefully. "I'm a Cornishman but I love England, too. My brother's in the Navy. He's fighting your U'Boats right now."

"Then I suppose I love Germany," Gerhard said. "But only if you invaded Friedsberg, my father's estate and where I grew up, could I really see you as the enemy."

I needed time to assimilate that. Busied myself in tearing up my own singlet, for I could see that the portions of his I had used to staunch his wound were now sopping red.

"This is daft, you know that? You got to have a doctor to cope with all this."

He nodded vacantly, obviously worlds away from his own wounds. "Last night in Buche-sur-mer, my fellow-officers and I celebrated my twenty-second birthday. Now I am talking with an English schoolboy in the heart of a forest. Life is indeed very strange. There is a poem of Heine . . . *Ich grolle nicht*."

That was the first German phrase I had heard complete from him. I thought he spoke the language much better than Herr Gottlieb. He closed his eyes once more and by the tightening at the corners of his mouth I sense that more pain was coursing through him. I had lost all fear of him now. Indeed, my one huge fear was of his dying.

"You must lie quiet and I will tell them at school and they will get you a doctor," I repeated dully — as if some rote words would be in themselves efficacious.

But this time what I was saying sunk in. He not only revealed those pale blue eyes again but sat up straighter. Even his voice was crisper than when he had uttered the German words. "No, Daffey, *please*! I ask only this of you. To leave me here until I feel better. *Do not tell anyone.*" He said that almost fiercely. When I made no reply he went on. "I promise you that if the wound in my back does not desist and if your nursing has not helped to halt the bleeding, I — I will surrender to the authorities. But please — not right away. That is what I am asking."

Oddly enough, my mind was not dwelling on or even following the contours of his request. Instead my thoughts were back at school: recalling the unfairness of obligatory sports, remembering that Ian McDermott and his snooty moral airs. I was persuading myself that I would do what this hurt German officer wanted because I liked him more than those things.

I think Gerhard, though, was thinking that I was in the process of denying his request. "Daffey, will you not tell them because we are fellow-naturalists?"

I smiled at that. Happy to agree. "I won't tell. I shall say I got lost in the woods and that is why I am late back. I shall tell them my singlet got torn to shreds on a bramble bush."

He lay back then. Right back. With his blond curls lying in the dirt of the forest floor. And he was speaking faintly again. I only just caught his words. "Come here, closer please."

I did as I was bid, putting my face close to his, if only to hear him better.

"You — you are an excellent nurse, my naturalist friend. You are a good boy, as well." With that he made a straining effort; lifted his head slightly and sealed my forehead with a kiss. His lips were very hot. I reared back embarrassed.

"I must go," I said quickly. "Or they'll come looking for me." I took one last sweeping look at that uniform with all its many items I would prize as souvenirs. I hesitated, wondering if I could dare ask . . .

"I have upset you with the kiss? You are too old for such things? Or is it because I am a German pilot and you a proud English schoolboy?"

"It's none of that," I told him truthfully. For after that first quick reaction I didn't mind too much. It was better than being smothered by all my aunts back in Cornwall when I went home for the holidays. "It's just that —" I broke off.

"Yes?" His voice was soft as well as faint.

"It's only that — well, *afterwards*. I'd like to tell my friends. And they aren't going to believe I actually met a Jerry — sorry — a German fighter-pilot in the forest unless . . . Well, unless I can prove it."

"So?" He was genuinely perplexed I think.

"Like a souvenir. A button or something?"

Realization dawned for Gerhard. He very slowly raised his one good arm and drew it across his chest. With a quick tug he tore his breast button free and held it out. It didn't have a swastika on it, but in my eyes, the second best thing: an unmistakeable German cross.

"Gosh, thanks!" I said. Then fearing he might change his mind or think I might rat on him and show it to a policeman, I started to leave.

"Goodbye Daffey. And thank you."

"Goodbye, Gerhard," I returned. "It was jolly interesting talking to you."

When I got back to school I went straight to my locker and put the button in there. After supper Mr. Hammond summoned me to his rooms and asked me why I had not signed in on the return from the cross-country. I told him I got lost in Mailton Woods and that when I eventually got back I couldn't find either him or the register.

"I despise all liars, Bryant, but when they are too lazy to even put some imaginative muscle behind their falsehoods, I consider it a personal affront. I shall now proceed to beat you six times instead of the three I had originally intended. Bend over."

After I had taken my punishment and was duly crying I repaired at once to my bed and locker. I took out my button which had now cost me six cutting strokes of the cane across the buttocks. I clenched it tightly and put my other hand to the place on my bottom which I imagined was already darkening from bruising and which I half-hoped was bleeding a bit. That joined me to Ober-Leutenant Gerhard Without-a-Surname, lying out there in the dark of the forest. The notion comforted me.

Charlie Lazarus came into our dorm, for his bed was adjacent to mine. I had slipped the button into my trouser pocket on hearing the door open, and was about to retrieve it and show him my trophy. But he spoke first.

"Heard the news, then?"

The one upsmanship in his voice was hard to take, but I knew he was pretty sure I hadn't or he would not have asked. "No I haven't. What news? Bloody war's over?"

"Danny Josephs and Ian McDermott went looking for you in Mailton Woods and guess what — they came across the body of a dead German. One of 'em that was fighting right over us on the cross-country, I suppose."

He stopped and looked hard at me. "What's the matter? You sick or something?"

With trembling fingers I played with the button in my pocket. "I must take a shit," I said to my friend. "See you later."

And when I was sitting in the cold dank of the bogs off our dorm, I started to cry again. But they were a different kind of tear, it was a different grief, from that which had welled in me when that old bastard Hammond had given me a beating.

# In
# The Mood

**O**n the November Saturday I have in mind, when I was fifteen plus and shaving hopefully once a week, the cinema had been censored by my Flanders-muddied father . . .

"Doesn't matter what you do say, Davey — you bain't g'in' to see no gangster film with all that shootin' and killin'. Let on 'em do what they loike with machine guns to Chicago, there b'aint no need to film on it. Sides, we had enough slaughter over to Europe the last toime, without going into some dark ole cinema to see some more."

"But Father, you don't *understand*. 'Tidn'n the same. This is Edward G. Robinson."

My mother gave the huge, cast-iron frying pan an extra shake. "Twouldn' make a bit of difference my dear, if 'twere the Bishop of Truro. Your father's roight."

"You bet your bloody loife I'm roight. There's enough muck in that boy's head without addin' a bunch o' they gangster films."

For once I didn't argue. When Father swore that meant finality. Anyway, I could sense they'd been talking about it ever since they'd seen the picture advertised in *The Cornish Guardian*. Probably one of their endless discussions in bed. I could guess, too, why they'd put off telling me to the very day I wanted to go. They were somewhat out of patience, shall we say, with the volume, the sheer staying power, I usually brought to my daily disagreements with them.

My fatalism on this occasion, as I stonily spooned my soup, was apparently interpreted as crushing disappointment, or maybe I even looked suicidal — a subject I'd brought up once or twice recently, especially since Tom Menheniot at school had went and hanged himself in his father's barn.

"It idn' the end of the world, you know, Davey." (I refused even to look up at my father.)

"I tell 'ee what, Davey."

I let my spoon handle drop heavily back into the pea soup. "What, Mother?"

"There's a dance down to the old school hall tonight, b'aint there? Why don' 'ee taike on your sister?"

"That's an idea, Son. 'Tis toime you took up a bit wi' the maids, you. Better than mopin' around here with your face in a book all the toime."

"I — I don't know how to dance," I began — so overwhelmed by the idea I wasn't sure whether I liked it or not.

"Mary will teach on 'ee, won't you, Dear?"

My sister was just bringing in the rabbit pie from the oven to where we sat. "If Davey do want Oi to. Anyways, he's light enough on his feet. He won't have no trouble steppin' out, you!"

I looked gratefully at her. "O.K. then. I'll wear my new sports coat. My Donegal tweed."

I spent much of that afternoon brushing my Sunday gray flannel pants and ironing their crease. The last hour before our departure I squeezed blackheads and several times changed the parting in my Brylcreamed hair.

As we walked, brother and sister, down the snaking gravel lane that divided Trehearne Meadows, the rain slackened and the edges of great black clouds sailing in from the coast took on the frosty lightness of a still invisible moon. Our feet clip-clopped loudly in the otherwise silent dark. Every now and then I looked fondly at kerchiefed Mary, pleased with her smart appearance, while my nose found her 'Bouquet of Violets' perfume, glamorous.

"What's the band like, they got down there, then? Not much for just a village 'hop I s'pose."

" 'Tis from Delabole — 'tidn' bad, Davey. Not considerin', that is."

"I — I suppose there won't be many there that I do know."

"You'll know plenty of the girls all right. Men's another matter," Mary added.

"Oh? How's that then?" Our shoes continued to clop together for a few paces.

"Well, for one thing there's the boys from up Davidstow airdrome. And there'll be sailors, probably — from the coastguard station at Tregardock Head. Then of course, there's the Yanks."

"They'd be from the American camp on top of Treyarnon Hill?" I asked.

"Roight enough! And they be darkies, too, moved in there, so Molly Pascoe told Oi. Good dancers, moind. But some on 'em is so black that it do take your breath away!"

I had never seen a black man. I had never seen an American, for that matter. Not close up, that is. I'd seen 'em in their great big white-starred lorries with their shapeless clothes and funny leather boots like old ladies' gaiters. And once — once into Bodmin I'd seen a group of them chewing gum and laughing louder than any of us would've done. They rolled down Nicholas Street with their strange way of walking — like there was some special joint between their thighs and their hips that we didn't have.

"Listen, Davey: *'You are my sunshine,'* " my sister sang, *"My only sunshine, You make me happy, When skies are gray, You'll never know, dear, How much I love you . . .'* " She nudged my elbow as she quickened pace to the dance tune so that our shoes didn't clack in unison any more.

Ahead lay the lych-gate and, finally, the moss-heaped, uneven roof of the ancient schoolhouse that was wedged between the narrow lane and the swirling, tumbling Amble River. Water still dripped from vestigial leaves, but over the spaced-out splashing and the noisy waters of the river below, came the sounds of the dance music — of piano and percussion, and the soft drool of a saxophone across the moist night air.

Inside the converted schoolroom the blast of the band behind its silvered, fretwork stands, contrasted strangely with the desultory dancing. Fred Trewin, stringy from TB, danced cheek to cheek with his newly-wed, the big-breasted Land Army girl in her green sweater uniform from up to St. Endellion. Molly Pascoe and Joan Jago from the post office half danced together, half fooled around. Each would have preferred a male partner but I could see that their slithering feet refused to wait for some uncertain invitation in a world of men at war.

Someone about my own age (I think from St. Teath where they all have rabbit teeth) with slicked-down hair and a gray, chalk-striped suit, swayed with a maid in a red dress from Wadebridge. I recognised her as the girl who sometimes flirted with me in the fish and chip shop where she worked.

And that was about it. Traces of french chalk to help the dancers still laced the rough floorboards on which my great-grandparents had sat at their desks, goodness knows how many years before. Mary and I were obviously early.

My sister left her coat in the tiny vestibule and put on her silvery dancing shoes. I didn't want any such commitment as hanging a coat up so draped my macintosh over the back of a chair near the exit. As I straightened up I nodded nervously towards a trio of boys from the village who stood isolated in one corner and who every now and then made low-voiced comments or catcalls to the dancers — comments that were rewarded by their mates with extravagant cackling and laughter.

"Good!" said Mary, joining me. "Most of 'em is still over at the inn. We can dance proper for once."

Self-conscious, gauche, I allowed her to pull me onto the floor. Sweating with fear, not heat, I followed her movements in a quickstep. Out of the corner of my eye I watched Molly and Joan doing what my sister described as 'that there a jitter-buggin'. I prayed that she had nothing similar in mind for me — and I sagged with relief when, after a couple of further dances (a St. Bernard's Waltz and a slow foxtrot), there came a thing called an 'Excuse me' and Jim Carthew from Pendoggett took my place and I could escape to the back.

Since we had arrived the hall had begun to fill. Indeed, as I turned gratefully towards the door and saw the burgeoning crowd, I was amazed at the transformation. The Cornish Arms must have run out of beer and cider, and closed its doors early, which wasn't all that surprising considering the wartime shortages. Either that or the dance was attracting a remarkable number of teetotallers. But I knew that was untrue as I mixed with the milling mob about the entrance; caught the breath of some and the slurred syllables of others.

Suddenly it was all rather exciting. Molly and Joan would no longer have to dance together, I realized, as I found myself surrounded by a variety of uniforms — mostly of khaki soldiers and blue airmen but with a navy-and-white sailor scattered here and there.

Slowly, for speed was out of the question, I edged my way towards the cramped foyer. I was then in the middle of a group of black American soldiers: softspoken and gum-chewing. For the most part girl-less, they just stood there, some of them with their backs to the wall as they quietly eyed the situation: uncertain in the alien Cornish environment, with an almost solid phalanx of British servicemen between them and the blaring gaiety of the dance floor.

At once I felt — well, to tell the truth, I felt several things. These were guests — in a special way, I mean — and yet they were being ignored. I felt shy, nervous even. They looked so very different with their exotic American uniforms and smooth faces. I noticed from a batch of new arrivals that several were wearing capes. It had obviously started to rain again.

My own raincoat was somewhere behind me — inside there on the back of a chair. But what was I thinking of? I had no real desire to go outside. We hadn't been there for much more than half an hour . . . where *did* I want to go then? I stared hard at the new faces, as if somehow one of them could provide an answer to these strange promptings.

"Why, if 'tidn' Davey Bryant! What be doin' out 'ere then, Boy? Fun's inside, b'aint it?"

It was Jim who worked for us on the farm. There wouldn't be

many more dances for him on Saturday nights for he had already received his call-up papers. Jim was a special pal of mine.

"Yes I s'pose, Jim," I said lamely. "Came out here for a bit of air. Tis as hot as hades in there."

But he must have sensed something. Then Jim would have. He could always tell my moods right away. I never had to tell him what had been going on with my family indoors, when I crossed the farmyard to join him for a forbidden cigarette in the stables.

"I'll go on in then, Boy. Take care, Davey. Don't 'ee do nothin' I wouldn' you!"

I nodded foolishly, not relaxing until his thickset body had disappeared into the throng. Now there were only black men about me. Not a white face. Wherever I looked and listened, the low American accents, the sweat-shining faces, white teeth and broad noses . . . My pulse quickened. Excited *and* frightened, that's what I was. The two emotions jostled in me as I made for the safety of the wall where the surge of the crowd was less.

"Pardon me, Boy." I arched my back out of the way as the never-ending concourse poured in from outside towards the makeshift coat-counter and the dance floor beyond.

I looked quickly up. Really up for he was tall. He stood there, back to the wall, very erect. The brown face impassive except for the eyes that caught my glance . . . held it. Instantly I turned away. My sight, that is. Otherwise I edged inch by inch toward the olive drab uniform. I had time to notice the upside-down sergeant's stripes on an arm, followed it down to where a brown thumb clung limply to the beginning of a trouser pocket.

All the half-thoughts, all the churning of mind, seemed at that point to retreat. A magnetism, whether from him or from within myself, I did not know, impelled me closer — until we were separated by no more than two or three feet. I licked my lips, prepared to lift my head again and say something — though having nothing to say; no word of excuse, no form of rationalization . . .

Circumstance suddenly delivered me. A new contingent drew near us from outside. Quickly I stepped towards him and turned around, my back now towards him. The crowd began to pass us and I was pushed even closer to him, so that if I strained upwards I could see his jutting chin. For awhile we were pressed one to the other and I experienced both release and tension. Release, somehow, in the *shelter* of him: tension in my trespass upon another's, a total stranger's, space.

The press slackened. Shifting towards the door I could see the tattered, mud-splattered black out material concealing the light of the vestibule in which we stood. In coldness the knowledge came to me that my excuse for standing there so close, was rapidly dissolving. And in the realization came the awareness I had no wish to move . . .

Was it my imagination or *did* he shift uneasily, feeling I was hemming him in? Panicky, yet even so with infinite caution, I dropped my hands behind me, gingerly explored the smooth texture of his uniform — not sure where my blind fingertips had embarked upon the deliberate geography of his body. The cloth was unwrinkled, tight-drawn. In a whisper of touch the backs of my nails informed me I was brushing his thighs. With hands loosely clasped behind me I lifted them, still gently, but with a new courage of firmness — for I'd already sailed from any safe harbor of retreat or explanation.

My eyes closed as I found what my loinal self so hungrily searched. I swayed, I think, in the vertigo of lust. With a caress as much informed by exhausted relief, as triumph, I boldly charted the width and length of his stiffening prick.

At about the level of my Brylcreamed hair there came from his chest the resonance of a voice unfurling. Deep, deep as his mahogany darkness and sending afloat in me the basso image of a glistening muscular torso in *King Solomon's Mines,* I heard in my movie-contoured mind, the voice of Paul Robeson transported to Cornwall. Above me, yet dropping as succinct and heavy pebbles through the waters of my consciousness, I heard the answer to my fumbling enquiry.

"You make a man ambitious, Boy."

But only my hidden hands spoke. I had no words.

He breathed heavily. "Let's go outside, huh?"

As he pressed in front of me it was not mere lack of balance that made me almost stumble. All I could do was nod my head as I prepared to obediently follow him. It was then I opened my eyes and drew breath to stop my trembling. It was as well I did so for moving quickly towards me was my sister, Mary.

From that day to this I have not known whether she saw me at that moment, about to leave with the tall Negro, for at the moment of recognition I dropped my sight and a novel composure encased me. Cunning, instant and cool, took me out of danger, took me away from the domestic association which I willed into extinction. But once more staring at the broad, army-clad shoulders of my sergeant as I followed in his wake, my cheeks, I knew, burned with embarrassment. I shared the sense of shame with the woman taken in adultery, pushed forward for the attention of Jesus.

The sense of the night air with its lacing of wetness, the enveloping dark, was a merciful gown to me as I stepped behind him away from the flare of light. For a few paces our feet crunched loudly below our preoccupied silence as we pursued the soggy gravel of the path.

"Got someplace to go, Boy?"

"No. Not really. I thought —"

The close-cropped head nodded, just below the bare branches of the dripping elms. "Somewhere down there, then, huh?" He pointed.

"Yes, I s'pose. 'Fraid it's a bit wet."

But I didn't really know where he was leading with his long, purposeful strides through the miserable night.

"This'll do, Kid."

We seemed to have walked a long way. I had no idea where I was. The smell of rubber was strong as he spread his waterproof cape on the grass slope, dropped down, pulling me along with him. More hearing than seeing, I knew he was unzipping clothes. Fumblingly I unbuttoned mine, kicking underpants down towards my ankles, so that I felt the abrupt chill of raindrops on my exposed buttocks.

At first he tried to enter me from behind but as I groaned

with pain he slackened his hold. In the release of his pressure I turned quickly over. It was then, in the faint light, under the hissing sky, I saw the hugeness of him. My head swam. My hand reached forward to clasp at his warmth, to fondle. Dimly I sensed the pressure of his hands at my head to force me closer, but even in the sweet humiliation of it came the involuntary jerking between my legs as my spending suddenly assailed me. I grew quiet as his needs grew stronger, his strength more affirmed.

"Go on, Boy. Take it!" In the slackness of me, I think his awareness sparked. "You're through, Boy, ain't you?"

I wanted to lie, to pretend — but no words at all would come. Abruptly he sat up. "You're just a kid, ain't you? You ever done this before? How old are you, son?" He was doing himself up, all casual and calm. I envied that.

"Me? I'm fifteen. That is, I'll be sixteen come January month."

"Crazy kid! I got a boy near so old as you. Back in Delaware."

"You have?" I thought I sounded as stupid as I felt.

"Guess I'm going to pick up one of dem chicks, Boy." He stood up. A black giant in the hissing rain. "S'long, Kid."

And that was that. I mean he was gone and I was there alone on the sodden turf. I turned over on my tummy and kicked the ground as a vicarious chastisement of myself. My foot touched stone . . . granite . . . For the first time since leaving the old schoolhouse I took notice of my whereabouts. Listlessly I pushed myself up by my hands until I was kneeling; not caring anymore about the clinging damp of my clothing or the cold wet to my knees. To my left was a mound, above it a headstone, and immediately beyond that, three yew trees. I knew where I was then all right . . .

Staggering a little, I got right up, moved to the tombstone where I had no need to strain in the dark to read the inscription. My Great-Uncle Petherick had carved and polished that granite slab; Father, himself, had planted those three young trees, when I was quite little, before the war. I had lain with my sergeant whose ambition I had excited — and so dismally failed to resolve — alongside the crumbling remains of my Great-Aunt Sarah who had died in her ninety-first year.

My hand went out to her slab to steady myself. I wanted to whisper something, to tell her . . . to try and explain. But instead, in my head, there grew an avenue of light, so fierce and sharp I had to blink my eyes to make sure it wasn't right outside there in the rain-lashed churchyard. I hurried down that light-path into a long-gone summer. I arrived — oh, it was just seconds away — at the sight of a hunched old lady wearing boy's heavy farm boots and clad from neck to mud-frayed hem in the green-black rustle of widow's weeds. She was carrying a milk bucket in her shaking, arthritic hand.

"Come to help of me, have 'ee, Davey?" Great-Aunt Sarah said. "You'm a good boy, me 'andsome! You be more full of love than all they others. Dear of 'un, then. Bless your little heart!"

In the release of self-pity the tears really came. Great-Aunt Sarah went back to her darkness under the yews. The rain came down fiercer than ever and I began to run. Wildly, heedless of ground consecrated or unconsecrated, I dodged between the mounds. Sending bedraggled grave-flowers scattering, I cried my way, zig-zagging over the dead. I ran until my chest heaved and the pain of the stitch in my side was sharper than my sense of failure towards Great-Aunt Sarah.

Finally, soaked to the skin, I arrived where I knew I must. At the entrance to the dance. As I entered, to a flurry of odd looks and murmurings, I searched frantically for Mary. But first, as people parted to allow a dampened Davey through their midst, I saw the sergeant. To the saxophone lilt of the *Chatanooga Choo-Choo,* he was dancing sinuously with Eileen Roscarrow from two farms over from ours. Her head lay dreamily below his shoulder. His left hand rested lightly on the small of her back as they sailed past. I noticed his fingertips were pink. I caught one glimpse of his eyes and was going to turn quickly away when I saw that they were half closed, his expression beatific . . .

"Davey — where the devil you been?"

"Oh, 'tis you, Mary. Oi've been looking all over for 'ee."

"Oi loike that! You looking for me! Why, 'tis the other way 'round! Now look on 'ee! You'm soaked. What's Mother g'in say?"

"I fell over — out there in the wet," I lied smoothly. "I went out for a drop of fresh air and there was someone lying on the ground. Drunk I s'pose. Anyways, I tripped and fell. You ready to go then?"

She hovered as always, my sister, between irritation and concern. "I don't know what's the matter with you, Davey, really I don't."

"Come on," I said. "Get your things. I'm not really in the mood for dancin' anymore."

# Return
## of
# The Native

It was late in February month that Danny told me all about him. There are two winters in Cornwall and Danny told me about the man who had come home, in the second one: the winter where cold never creeps, where the long ferns (though limply hanging from the mossy stone hedges) stay green from the previous summer, and where primroses star as neighbors to white and blue violets. The other winter informs the contrary uplands of twisted blackthorn and leafless oaks where swollen sheep with rain-rank fleeces refuse to yield lambs to the frost-white turf.

The man's home, long and rambling, with an uneven roof of whitewashed slates, we cycled past daily on our way to school. But until Danny took me aside one school dinner-time and told me as he munched the pasty his mother had packed him, about Petherick Clemo and his home, I'd never given a thought to the wisteria-festooned house, half-hidden in the foliage of enormous fig bushes that we passed at the foot of Tregear Hill. That was an incline which we sped down furiously each day in our efforts to turn the bend and pedal the following slope as far as possible before having to dismount.

Although Danny Coad lived only two farms over from ours, he was a fairly new friend. For one thing he had switched from Camelford School the previous autumn and for another I had just been advanced a form so it was January that had seen us for the first time in the same class. Almost a year older than me, at seventeen he had something of a reputation in our village of Pentinny. Already six foot and boasting the need to shave twice a day, he lived in an aura of ogling girls, of blue cigarette smoke and of beer on his breath at weekends. I didn't exactly *like* Danny but I was both intrigued by him and attracted to him. He was always telling me new things — without ridiculing my ignorance. And watching his long brown body dancing about the gymnasium when he put on the gloves and beat every comer, or seeing him grab the muddied rugby ball and speed as a wing three quarters down the churned field to score a try, I felt proud to own his friendship. Rather like owning your first 250 cc motor-bike I suppose, or, as I used to visualize him in bedtime fantasies, like being a brilliant dictator of some Balkans country whose personal fears could be dissolved in a muscular bodyguard.

It was a Monday in February that I sat on the bank in the noonday sun, watching him through the lashes of half-closed lids — so that he appeared just a darkish haze in a sea of blurred orange. He was sitting on the grass below me — obviously impervious to the worms my mother swore would enter one if ever the human bottom met cold stone or damp ground.

"Here, Davey, I got an idea. Want to do something on the way home from school, you?"

I opened my eyes, just in time to see him spit out a bit of gristle from the pasty beef and fling the knotted pastry end into the air for the crying gulls that wheeled hungrily overhead. "Such as?"

"Just someone I do know who'd like to meet 'ee." He cocked his rather small head on one side — like an intelligent terrier. His black hair thatching his swarthy complexion, was almost metallic in the sunlight. "C'mon, Davey. 'Twouldn' take long. An' I reckon you'll thank me afterwards, too."

A vision of Mother first stooping over the kitchen range to bring out bright yellow saffron buns (promised) and then laying tea, dispersed with gratifying speed.

"Well, 'tis Joseph's job to help Father wi' milking . . . All right, I don't see why not. I musn't be late, moind. 'Twould be hell to pay at home if Oi'm late again for tea."

"That's up to you, idn' it? 'Tis you what got to live wi' 'er — Oi 'aven't."

Relief mixed with smugness in his voice and I looked away in embarrassment. Two farms over was only three fields distance from Tregellis, where he lived, to our place. I knew very well how her nagging cries travelled those leafless winter days . . . Those railings at me and my brother Joseph each morning before we left for school; the hysterical calls for my father who had already retreated upfield — to do tasks beyond the scope of her emaciated, arthritic body. But it was all *our* sadness, our clannish tensions. In the sunken solitude of Tregarrow farm, surrounded by elms, screened by ivy and periwinkle, it was bearable: part of the pain of being a Bryant and as inevitable as the farming rhythm itself. But the knowledge of it bounced back from an *alien* mouth, was a searing thing against which I had no defense.

As we left the highway atop Pender Hill and sped the winding Cornish lanes, sailed single file across the narrow humped bridges that spanned each tiny inlet of the Camel estuary, I prayed that Danny had not spoken of us Bryants to this Petherick Clemo I was about to meet for the first time.

We dismounted at the foot of Tregear Hill. "Is — is he expecting me, Danny?"

"I said as how I moight bring a friend along. He do know all about 'ee. I told of 'ee that down to school, didn' Oi?"

With that I had to be content. I licked dry lips and hoped for the best, feeling nervous as always at the thought of strangers.

"Don't leave your bike out there by the hedge. He do loike on 'em left *inside*. That way there b'aint no-one do know who's a visitin' of 'un or no."

As Danny held the small white gate open with his foot, I looked along the narrow, flagstoned path that ran the length of the house. Green shutters about upstairs windows contrasted sharply with the whitewashed stone; a long, glassed-in verandah, beyond which I could see wicker garden furniture, was semi-screened by partially lowered venetian blinds —

presumably against the straw sunlight of early evening.

There was something faintly exotic about the outside of Petherick Clemo's house. With the luscious vegetation of sprouting bamboo and evergreen rhododendrons that billowed heavily on the fringe of the trim lawn, I thought of Colonial Residences in far-off tropical places. I was soon to learn that the impression was one deliberately simulated. It was certainly intensified when a plumpish man, I guess in his fifties, suddenly appeared as I propped my bike next to Danny's against the wall. He was wearing spotless white ducks and a cream-colored polo neck sweater above them. A beige beret sat squarely on his head and below hornrimmed glasses a set of evidently false teeth were clearly revealed by a broad grin.

His voice was husky — with just a suspicion of an accent I couldn't identify. He shouted to Danny, ignoring me. "That you, Danny? I see you have brought your young friend, huh?"

Danny came up by my side, after bolting the door, I noticed, which led to the small gate and the hill beyond. "Don't act so surprised, then. You made Oi promise, didn't 'ee?"

"Nothing of the sort, you young shit. I just said that if the one with nice curly hair came past again with you, to bring him in for a cup of tea."

This exchange took place from either side of the glass partition of the verandah but just as, in a rare gesture, Danny put his arm about my shoulder, our host came out to the path and stood before us. He had collected a loose-knit shawl which I had noticed draped over one of the chairs, and now wore it about his shoulders.

"Yes, that's the one. I won't tell you the number of times I've seen him turn that corner at the foot of the hill. Got a brother, haven't you? About the same age? You always used to be together. He had curly hair — but not as nice as yours."

"That 'ud be my brother Joseph. He's a year younger than me, though."

"Is that so? Well, Danny here seems to be monopolozing you these days — though we'll put a stop to that if we can."

"My brother leaves school half an hour earlier than us. He goes home now with Dennis Carhart from Treblaze."

He suddenly shivered. "Come on, boys. Let's go on the stoop. I'll get another attack of my damned asthma if we stay out here."

"B'aint no one keepin' us," Danny told him, giving my shoulder a reassuring squeeze.

"Why did I come out here for in the first place, then? Oh yes, now I remember! The introductions." A cool, dry hand came out to pump mine. "Danny will've told you, I'm sure. I'm Petherick Clemo. No need to tell me who *you* are. Davey Bryant from Tregarrow."

"Yes, that's roight enough, Maister."

"Come on in, then." And from over his shoulder as he led the way. "Brother of Joseph and son of Arthur. You and your brother take after your mother in looks, I've always felt, what with that curly hair and those gray eyes. And by the way, I think that cousin of yours from St. Endellion looks like an angel when I see him each Sunday in the choir. Now sit yourselves down and I'll make the tea. I can hear the kettle boiling."

And he was gone. I sat down on a chair opposite Danny and looked about me. A large bowl of growing blue hyacinths filled the air with scent. Behind where Danny sat were bookshelves to the ceiling while more books were scattered on occasional tables, on the sofa next to Danny and even on the floor.

"Well, what do you think of 'un? Funny ole bugger, eh?"

"He — he must've read a lot," I said. "He's got bravun many books."

"You b'aint seen nothing. Inside is worse. Stacked from floor to ceiling wherever 'ee do go. He don't go out in winter, see, with his asthma. So he spends of his toime readin'. That's when there b'aint the loikes on *us* to take up his toime."

"I see," I said, not seeing at all. Danny took his jacket off. He seemed very much at home. I thought that he must visit there pretty often to act as if he owned the place.

"Relax," Danny said. "You be sitting as if 'ee be waitin' for the dentist."

"Is — is there a Mrs. Clemo?"

"You kiddin'?" With that Danny leaned over and took a cigarette from an oriental-looking box — made of lacquer I think. "Want one?"

"No thanks. I —"

"Yes?"

I had been about to say that Mother would've smelt the tobacco on my breath as soon as I'd entered the back kitchen. But Danny wasn't a person I told things like that to. "Nothin'. Just wonderin' what he do do, that's all. Nice place he's got here."

"He don't do nothing. Retired. Man o' leisure ole Petherick is." With that Danny raised his legs from the floor and stretched them along the sofa: something I would never have dared do back at Tregarrow.

"I b'aint never heard anyone mention him 'cept you. 'Tis funny that. You usually hear about people, don't you?"

"You would if 'ee lived over here to Pentithy. Moind you, he b'aint been here that long. Eighteen month I reckon."

"Eighteen months since I got *back*," Petherick Clemo corrected, appearing with a large silver salver with the tea things on it. "Now stop telling my story for me, Danny. Davey and I will play question and answer on our own. You don't like tea, anyway. Why don't you go and have a bath, eh?"

Danny jumped off the sofa. "Reckon I will. This is one at least I can have in peace." Then to me: "Keep him talkin', will 'ee, Davey? Otherwise he'll be climbin' they stairs so soon as he hears Oi splashin' in his tub."

Grinning like an idiot, wholly at a loss for words, I nodded vaguely and for something to do with my embarrassed hands, picked up the nearest book from the wicker table next to me. It was a small red volume. The author's name: Edward Carpenter.

Danny departed but Petherick Clemo didn't address me. Instead he plonked himself down on the spot Danny had just started to warm, and eyed me steadily. I knew it but kept looking at the book, flicking its pages.

Finally he gave in. "Like reading do you, Davey? Ever read that one?"

"No," I said, closing the covers. "No, I haven't."

"You can take it with you if you like. But don't let Mother see it. Somehow I don't think it's the kind of book she'd approve of."

"What's it about then?"

"It's called *Friendship* isn't it? Well, the clue is in the title."

"'Bout friends, then? That it?"

"In the sense of brotherhood, yes. You know the word *frater-nity*?"

"Like people — men — belonging to something? Some association or club maybe?"

"Exactly. Anyway, we'll come to that later."

"You live alone here then? Not married or anything?" It took a lot of effort for me to ask all that. I sighed heavily.

"Come on," he responded lightly. "Don't be nervous. I'm not going to bite you, you know. No, I'm not married. I returned to Cornwall when my mother was dying. Then came the War and I couldn't get away even if I'd wanted to."

"You was living abroad then, that it?"

"You name it — I've lived there. A real old Cousin Jack I was — the proverbial Cornishman overseas. And a wild time I had, too." He looked at me over his glasses. "You will too, I can tell."

"Have a wild toime?"

He laughed. "That as well if those good looks keep up. But I was thinking of the wandering. You have a restless spirit, I can tell. Knew it from the minute you walked in. I'm psychic."

"I don't know what that is."

"Psychic? Able to get right through to the spirit — move out of word range into the mystery of things."

He sounded like a schoolmaster when he spoke like that. But I liked it. He told you what you wanted to know. Quickly, without any fuss. Most teachers I knew were long-winded.

"Like to see a bit of the house while the tea's brewing? Got several things which might interest you?" He got up from his seat with considerable less alacrity that Danny had displayed. On his feet he wheezed and coughed chestily several times.

"Fucking asthma."

That immediately emboldened me. "Fuckin' weather don't help, I s'pose." I looked at him quickly, afraid that he might laugh at my cussing. He didn't seem to notice.

"Come on, I'll show you a few of my treasures. The books can wait until later. You can't look at them and talk at the same time. Though people try often enough."

I followed him through into a long, book-lined hallway with a bumpy slate floor, covered here and there with sheepskin rugs. He didn't pause for me but passed a door opening into the kitchen and finally in through a door at the end of the passage. Already I was keenly aware of the more sophisticated aura to his house than ours possessed, but his study, as the end room proved to be, was impressive enough to render me quite mute.

"I call this my den," he said, indicating a yellow-silk chaise longue for me to recline on, "but our Danny who is currently luxuriating in my expensive bath oils upstairs, calls it my web. I wonder what you will end up calling it." As he sat down in an armchair opposite me he looked enquiringly in my direction, again over the tops of his glasses.

Licking dry lips I cleared my throat. "Well, you don't look much like a spider," I managed.

"Bears live in dens, of course." He had already turned to a small table at his side and was wiping a silver-framed photograph he had taken from it, with the sleeve of his cardigan.

"Perhaps bear would be more like it, then," I said, feeling somewhat daring.

"Bears hug, of course." That came more quietly from him; soft enough for my pulse to quicken.

The room in which we now sat was different from the more open and airy verandah space. Looking further about me I became aware that on the flat surfaces of furniture, on the walls and on the lower shelves of built-in bookcases, were a multitude of photographs. Although the light was rather dim — for shutters screened the french windows leading to the slope of the lawn — I could see they were all oldish. The silver frames of them were old-fashioned, heavily ornamented, and those close to me showed foxing. Some had turned sepia with their white mounting almost yellow. Petherick Clemo handed me the photo-frame he had been dusting with his sleeve.

"I look less like a bear there, don't you think? Though I don't think 'spider' is a necessary alternative."

I was looking at the slim figure of a young man in tropical clothing. He was extraordinarily handsome as he stood by some kind of exotic tree with huge, banana-like leaves. "Is that you, then?"

"Who'd you think it was?" I looked up. His voice sounded somewhat rougher.

"Like — like you've changed," I muttered.

"I don't feel so," he wheezed angrily. "Just this damn asthma and all this Cornish stodge we eat."

"Where was that took to, then? Tis not Pentithy, that's for certain."

"I shan't call you a genius for that observation. It's Travancore, India. Spent some of the happiest years of my life there." He was already taking another framed photo from its perch and giving it a wipe.

I looked harder at the one I held. One hand of the figure was held knuckled at the waist, the legs slightly apart while the smiling expression radiated confidence. I wondered what he was smiling at with those full lips stretched so wide.

"What you grinning at then?"

"I was twenty-one. That's a smiling matter in itself, if you did but know it."

Strange things moved in me. I liked that face with its curved dark eyebrows below brown hair that fell in a wavy lock to one side. I stared harder, experiencing a weird desire to step through the dust-speckled glass. It was sunshine beyond, sunshine and warmth, and a nice face laughing. I glanced quickly towards the window, towards the moist and dripping mildness of a Cornish February day . . . then at the lined, bespectacled, oval sitting opposite me. Oh give me that *other* life, that *other* person, that *other* place, any day! But I said nothing. I had never really looked at old photographs before — at least, not any that had interested me very much. The only one I recalled at that moment was one of Grandfather Bryant's family, all whiskered and stern outside our farmhouse. There were no smiles there and you couldn't tell what kind of day it was.

He fed me the next one, taking the first from me and kissing it before replacing it on the shelf. There was an abrupt twitch in me. I, too, had been tempted to press my lips to that cool glass.

The second picture was of a group of young men, again in old-fashioned clothes, and all of some white material that seemed suited for the tropics. I looked carefully and could see the young Petherick Clemo standing between the other two. His arm was about the neck of one while the third rested against a cane. The one with the malacca cane was wearing a broad-brimmed hat. I thirsted over every detail.

"They were two of my very best friends in Delhi," my host informed me. "That beautiful thing with the dark hair was the Viceroy's P.P.S. My God! Delhi was a wild place in those days. Life was just one long orgy."

"Was it?" I asked, full of interest. I scrutinized the trio even harder, but I could read no extravagantly wicked thing there — just a group of young men, more handsome than most I thought, deciding for a lark, perhaps, to have their picture taken. Well, that and the other quality it shared with the photo of Petherick on his own — of another age and in a dead and different sunshine.

"Where be they now?" I asked. "Still out to India?"

"Larry, that's the dreamy thing with the malacca cane — he was killed in Capetown just after the Great War. They found his body near some kind of bazaar. He was murdered."

I stared intently at Larry again. The notion that I was looking at the face of a dead man appealed powerfully to me. I felt I could see the sadness of death in those eyes . . . . Finally satisfied I looked up.

"And t'other, then? What happened to he?"

"Reginald Folden? That one took to drink. Probably crawling about in the dirt of some fly-blown place like Dar-es-Salaam, if he's still with us. I've got some other photos of old Reggie — in quite different poses. I'll show 'em to you one day. But no one sees my special collection on their first visit, you understand?"

Like a huge cloud that wasn't there I felt the presence of insinuation in that memory-crowded room. It made me uncomfortable and I actually touched my forehead just to see whether it was as hot as I suddenly felt. I wished Danny would come back. I began to wish I hadn't come.

"Penny for 'em?" he asked. "Or shall I guess what you're thinking?"

The sweat was running from the palms of my hands and I hated their clamminess. "Bit hot in here, idn' it? Moind if I do go out there for a breather?"

"Make yourself at home. I'll go back and pour that tea. Close the bloody windows after you go or I'll be joining Larry and probably old Reggie."

I didn't even wait to see him rise from his armchair but hurried to the french windows and let myself out. The fresh air was elixir and I breathed deep. Dusk stirred about the lower boughs of the rhododendron bushes and I listened to the song of a sleepy blackbird hidden somewhere in the massed foliage bordering the wide lawn. As I stood there I tried to make understandable patterns of the gusts of anxiety that Petherick Clemo's presence sent through me.

Now, of course, I speak from hindsight, but even as I recall that birdsong under a rain-exhausted sky, can smell the damp loam of a bulb-sprouting garden and hear the rumble of Danny's bathwater sluicing away somewhere above my head, I relive the sensation of unease, flicked with irritation, that the encounter with Petherick Clemo had sparked.

But I was not left long in the cool of that early evening, striving to come to terms with myself. Suddenly a sash window clattered upwards and I turned to see Danny's head emerge through a billow of steam.

"What the hell be 'ee doin' out there? Go on back in for Christ's sake!"

"He — he said I could. He went to pour the tea . . ."

"I wouldn' have brought on 'ee here if I'd knew'd you was going to act like a bloody baby."

My eyes filled with tears. "I — I didn't think you was going to leave Oi for a bath roight away."

"Don't start blubberin' then." The roughness left his voice.

"Go on in. Oi'll be roight down. Go *on* now!" The window was yanked down again.

With knuckles dashed swiftly at both eyes, I shuddered a sigh and did as I was told. I managed to streak down the hall where I had first sat, and flung myself down before Petherick entered from the kitchen carrying a plate of buttered splits and lemon-curd tarts.

"Good," he said, as he handed me a cup of milkless tea and then a little jug. "It probably isn't totally cold. And I've brought fresh hot water in case it needs warming up."

Loathe to speak lest my voice revealed a break or an irrepressible sob, I reacted with nods and a forced smile as I took the milk, then the hot water and finally started to munch fiercely from the pile I had collected on my outstretched plate.

"Danny's coming roight down," I said with my mouth full, "he told me through the window. He's finished bathing."

"He has, has he? Changed the routine, then. Probably in your honor."

I didn't know what he was talking about but I certainly wasn't going to ask. As it turned out I didn't have to for Danny came in just then.

"There you are!" his host commented. "That was much quicker than usual. Dried your back on your little own, then?"

"Oi suddenly felt hungry. Here, let's have some o' they, afore 'ee do hog 'em all." Danny scooped two scones from the plate and crammed a whole one into his mouth. When he next spoke he sprayed crumbs. "You two gettin' on all roight? Have 'er got to all that art stuff yet, Davey? Ole Petherick's bravun good on that, b'aint 'ee?"

"You're too ignorant to know if I am or not," said Petherick cheerfully. "In any case, we haven't gotten any further than photographs."

"Oh, *they*." Danny leered meaningfully at me. "Got off to a good start wi' that lot. 'Cos Pethy here can't help being a dirty ole man — you realize that, I hope."

"It — they — were just some of him and his friends. Like that one behind you in the frame," I explained quickly.

"Your friend appreciates *nostalgia*, Danny. That's something far beyond your scope."

"He would like somethin' foreign. I told 'ee he were that way, didn' Oi?"

"You suggested he was a cut above the average Cornish oaf, if that's what you mean. Not that I've got anything against oafs — in certain contexts, that is."

I was beginning to feel neglected. "I'd like to see some more photographs. I only saw the two."

"He've got more interestin' ones than they, 'aven't 'ee, Pethy?"

Our host drained his tea cup then wiped his lined mouth daintily with a napkin from a pile I now noticed for the first time on the tray besides him. At home we only used them on Sundays. "There's lots of things to show Davey. All in good time, Danny, all in good time."

With Danny sitting there, low on his chair, his legs sprawled out before him, a slightly sulky look on his face, Petherick then proceeded to show me a series of old photos of himself and his friends, taken all those years before. Some of them again in India, a few in the Canadian Rockies, but most of them it seemed in South Africa where, he told me, he had spent many years of his much-traveled life.

Some of them were formal portraits; close-ups of handsome heads with an emphasis, I thought, on gentle eyes and full lips. The beauty of these moved me considerably. I thought of those I knew in our village, at school, of people I passed on the narrow streets of Wadebridge — and could think of none who approached the lovely features of these faces I now scrutinized so closely.

Others were snaps: a carefree snatching of lost moments in unknown places . . . Laughing, fooling youths without a care in the world, and in a *doux*, not a *dour* place — where palm trees leaned over a sparkling sea, not where angular blackthorn was twisted grotesquely by gales from a storming Atlantic.

When I put the last one down, one of my famous sighs escaped me. "Gosh — what you want to come back here to Cornwall for? I'd bravun love to live in a place like that — wouldn' you Danny?"

No reply. I looked around quickly. Only Petherick still sat there, eyeing me quizzically as I made a careful pile of the pictures examined, at the foot of the chaise-longue.

"Danny got bored," he said. "He always does if he isn't the center of attention. He's off in my bedroom, I expect — probably looking at my other collection of photographs and playing with himself at the same time."

I couldn't hide the intensity of my blush.

"What's the matter? Everyone does it, don't they?"

I hung my head. "I — I s'pose," I said thickly.

"Or maybe you aren't old enough?"

"Yes I am." I stopped; realizing just how neatly he'd caught me. But then, as I looked up and our eyes met, something odd happened. He winked at me. That's all. No other gesture. No words. And suddenly I didn't care.

"I do it all the time," I said, tilting my chin.

He took off his glasses and started to clean them with a large and rumpled handkerchief. "I don't disbelieve you for a moment. What do you think of?"

But that was beyond the capacity of my frankness. "'Tis none of your business."

When he made no reply I worried about sounding too rude. "I — I jest don't loike questions about that."

"How old are you, Davey?"

"Me? I'm sixteen. Seventeen come August."

"You're young aren't you? Young for your age I mean."

I thought for a moment. "Maybe sometimes I sound stupid. The words don't always come out roight. But I b'aint a fool exactly. I do know what's going on. Every bit as much as Danny, come to that."

"Well what *is* going on, as you put it. You think that something is going on here?"

But I wasn't going to be caught twice. I just stared back at him without speaking.

"You afraid of me, Davey?"

"No. Should Oi be then?"

"There's some would be. I've got quite a reputation in this village."

"Well, it isn't my village, is it?"

"Reputations don't stop at parish boundaries. Tell me, what did Danny tell you about me?"

"Nothin'. What did 'ee expect him to tell Oi?"

"That I was a bachelor. That I liked being visited by young people — young men that is."

I slid off the chaise-longue. "'Tis toime I was on my way home, Maister," I said. "I got to help Father with milkin'," I fibbed. "Thank you very much indeed for the tea and that."

He rose too. "We'll collect Danny on the way out. You coming to visit me again, Davey?"

On my feet I felt all right again. "Why not? It's on the way home from school, isn't it?"

"Would you like to borrow a book after you've had a browse 'round? We can discuss that next time you come."

"Yes I would," I said evenly. "I love reading. I'd loike to get through all these." I waved at his walls.

"You shall," he said over his shoulder as he led the way. "You shall."

I did . . . .

# All
# At Sea

"**W**e're putting you in D.E.M.S. You'll like that, Ops. It's a cushy number." The Chief Petty Officer at the Royal Naval Barracks, Devonport, gave me a wink. I sighed, assuming it to be as lewd as most of the others I had been accorded during my three months in the Navy. Then I was a seventeen-year-old Ordinary Seaman with an educated accent and rather girlish features . . . what else were those hoary young veterans, tired of bombardment, tired of being rescued from ice-cold waters, tired of World War bloody Two, to think?

When your wife is somewhere else and the sap of life flows vigorous under navy blue serge, a fresh-cheeked boy from a Cornish farm who is still naive enough after three months in The Service, to bend down and look for 'the golden rivet', supposedly somewhere embedded in the deck, is worthy of a whole lot more than lewd winks, or the quick fondling of buttocks as he stands in line for this or that.

But it wasn't just the endless series of sexual signals being flashed in my direction that bothered me at that particular moment. If my time in the Royal Navy since the January of 1944, when I stopped in the middle of winter ploughing and started my basic training at H.M.S. Royal Arthur, had been one of unmitigated sexual pressures, it had also been equally onerous as a time of learning a mystifying and quite unprecedent new language. The arcane vocabulary of the King's Naveey (otherwise referred to as 'The Andrew') had previously floored me with such sartorial gems as 'fore-and aft-rig' for my bell-bottom uniform, 'square rig' for those wearing collar and tie, and titfer for our little round hats with their H.M.S. tallybands. Those with sexual connotations were also legion: 'bash' or 'oppo' for chum or protege; a 'brown hatter' was the commonest term for a homosexual, while 'navy cake' was, to put it bluntly, a piece of ass. I may add that there were dozens of others which I was concerned to comprehend then, but which, in the thirty subsequent years which have brought me to this Canadian land of quite different dialects, I have long since forgotten or confused.

At the moment in time to which I now refer, when confronting the 'Chiefy' the new term was D.E.M.S. He must have read my frown of incomprehension. Another wink plus, this time around, an extravagant leer from those bright red lips above his black and bushy beard. "D.E.M.S.? That's Defensively Equipped Merchant Ships. It's a special number. Just a bunch of matelots swinging the lead or some merchantman what thinks it needs some of us from The Andrew to protect it from Jerry. What I've got for you, Ops, is a berth on our ocean-going tug out of Plymouth, The Recovery. There'll be just the three of you. The other two is old mates of mine who've been dipped in the oggy once too many times on the Atlantic convoys. For them it had to be either a nice cushy number like this — never out of Guz for more than two or three days at a time — or the psychiatric ward over there at the hospital. It's like a paid rest-cure what the navy puts on for a few from the Lower Deck what's in danger of getting waterlogged. Of course the bleedin' officers get provided with official cunt from the Wrens — and sent to Convalescent homes in the country." I looked at the N.C.O. with considerable suspicion. "Why *me* then? I've never done convoy duty or been torpedoed. I volunteered last week for transfer to the Fleet Air Arm. I want to be a pilot."

"Do you, now! How nice! Well, transfer from one branch of the Service to another takes time, Son. And this transfer to D.E.M.S. is right quick. Like you report today. The lads will be waiting for you. I promised 'em something nice, see. You'll be joining Leading Hand Rice and Able-Seaman McBridge. You'll kind of make up for what they aren't getting from the Women's Royal Naval Service, what's full of bloody snobs. Only the Recovery ain't no Convalescent Home, as you'll soon find out."

The Chief Petty Officer reached out for my barracks card which lay on the desk before him, and stamped in large, red initials, the letters D.E.M.S. right across it.

"What you looking so glum for, Bryant? You're going to *like* the Killock, Leading Hand Rice and A.B. McBride. They'll be the only protection you got between yourself and that stinkin' civvy crew. Those buggers got the morals of monkeys."

As I left the Administration Building in the direction of the dockyard where the Chief Petty Officer had ordered me to report, I walked more slowly than was circumspect within the purlieus of the Royal Naval Barracks — or 'Guz' as its occupants called it. The idea of further harassment for the unwilling favors of my teen-age body by two probably repulsive-looking old sailors didn't really depress me any more than a thousand and one other manifestations of this brutal, mechanized, and depersonalized world which offended every innate attribute I possessed. But the idea of moving now into a further realm — without even familiar emblems, evoked not so much distaste, as fear.

Yes, I walked slowly, not as a reluctant victim to a virtually promised rape, but because I was frightened of confronting anything freshly unknown. In the space of a single farm season — I had left before finishing the ploughing of Poltinny Meadow and the dredge corn in there would still be just short and green — I had achieved a total surfeit of anything new. If I had even glanced at something as familiar as a photograph of my mother I would have simply broken down there in the concrete wilderness of the barracks and bawled my eyes out.

When I reached the D.E.M.S. hut on the quay it was to find Leading Seaman Rice and Able-Seaman McBride waiting for me — or rather, for whomever Chiefy had been pleased to send them. That there had been a discussion of the matter was immediately evident.

Leading Seaman Rice, or 'the Killock' as the navy slang had it, was dressed in his 'number threes,' that is to say, his working uniform. He was the taller of the two, with straight, straw-colored hair which he wore brushed straight back without a parting. The red anchor, betokening his rank, stood out on the arm of his serge jumper which was both worn and carefully darned. He was smoking a hand-rolled cigarette, made from the Navy's official, duty-free tobacco, and balanced the mottled thing in the corner of his mouth as he spoke with his faintly Welsh accent.

"Come over 'ere, McBride and see what Chiefy's sent us. Hello then, Ops. I reckon you must be the little O.D. that's been sent to join us on The Recovery, eh?" His tone was even; not, I felt, insinuating.

"Yes I am," I told him. "I'm Davey Bryant and this is my first number since I got through basic training. I have been hanging around barracks for weeks."

At which point A.B. McBride arrived to inspect me. I took the opportunity to size him up, too. He was stocky and because of the sleeveless overalls he was wearing, I could readily perceive the powerful muscles about his shoulders and forearms. He had black, curly hair and spoke with a distinct Scots accent. He was later to tell me that he was born and raised in The Gorbals, the slums of Glasgow. But he did not have that runtish look or bad teeth that I had soon come to recognize among so many of the wartime sailors from the various slums and depressed areas of the British Isles. McBride had even white teeth which you couldn't help noticing because he smiled so much of the time.

"Davey Bryant — you a Janner then, Ops? Always munching tiddly oggies, are you?" 'Janner' was one of the first bits of naval slang I had learned. It meant a Cornishman (because we used Jan often as a firstname) and tiddly oggy (God knows why!) was a reference to our national dish, the Cornish pasty.

"Yes, from over near Padstow. How did you know?"

"One thing — you *look* like a Janner. Then your name. Davey. That's reet from ole Cornwall, I bet. Tons of Bryants here in Guz. I knew one of them — he was not as cute as you, though!"

"McBride will show you what's what," Leading Seaman Rice informed me. "And then you'd better get your gear from the barracks and get it down here. We sail at four today. I'm going up to the office, McBride. That prick of a Sub-Lieutenant, the new boy Watson, wants to see me."

When Rice had left, the affable McBride quickly filled me in as to the operation for which we were responsible. When the salvage tug, Recovery, to which we were assigned, was in port, we stayed there in the D.E.M.S. hut. It was there we kept the strip Lewis gun, which together with a rifle was the tug's only armament when at sea; and the crates of ammunition in canvas bags with which to feed the machine gun.

We lived quite apart from the routine of the barracks in that spic and span hut. Our hammocks were stashed at one end and there was a simple wooden table at which we could eat — we had our own adjacent galley where, McBride told me, he had done all the cooking but which he would now share with me. There was a couple of beaten-up armchairs and an ancient radio. Another of my jobs, he told me, would be to keep our accomodation ship-shape-and-Bristol-fashion. That would involve a complete scrub-out each morning with the aid of a squeegee. I didn't mind hearing that from McBride. I found physical work the best relief there was from the mental strains of naval regimented life.

I decided that morning, scurrying with my kitbag and hammock from the main barracks to my new home, that I quite liked McBride. Over the Killock, Rice, I was uncertain. Then I had seen much less of him. Later that afternoon, though, I was to discover that McBride tended to be much more the practical joker when in the presence of his fellow-rating and friend.

I was making sure my hammock was lashed tight enough with the customary knots to ensure it would float adequately if events determined it might be needed upon the surface of the sea, when McBride called across the room to me.

"Heh, Ops! Would you give me a hand, darlin! I've got me hands all messed up from greasin' this gun. Come over here, will ye?"

Dutifully, I did as I was bid. When I reached him he grinned forlornly, lifted his eyebrows and raised his hands.

"Got a bit of a problem, Matey. Help me out, will ye, Bash?"

I eyed his sweaty arms and grimey hands. "What do you want me to do?"

"In my pocket. Could ye put your hand in and get me cigarette case out?"

I vaguely wondered why he bothered with a cigarette case as, unlike Rice, he didn't smoke 'ticklers' from which the tobacco was always falling out if you weren't careful. But it never crossed my mind to defy that friendly face.

My hand went into the slit of his dungarees where he helpfully proferred his right hip in my direction. I quickly sought the metal shape of his cigarette case. In what must have been mere seconds — but what seemed like aeons — I learned first, that he was wearing nothing under his over-alls, and second, that what my hand grasped was not cold metal but warm, cylindrical flesh. And even as my fingers blindly encircled its width before jerking away as if in contact with something whitehot, he let out a scream of mirth.

"Oh me darlin' I didna know ye cared! Heh, Rice," he shrieked, "Ye can have the chile's sister, like ye said. I'll stick wi' what I got!"

My hand darted back to my side — but not soon enough to modify in any way the doubled-up hilarity of the two of them. This was patently a routine which they tried out on every unsuspecting victim who was dumb enough to be lured into searching for that mythical cigarette case through a slit which led not even to underwear but direct to McBride's manhood.

I smiled sheepishly but took care not to seem sullen or put out. I had already learned that with these war-scarred matelots, the line between boisterous humor and something more akin to bullying was a thin one. On this occasion they took my smile at face value and offered no more sexual allusions in my direction. Shortly thereafter we were gathering up our kit and armament material, preparatory to boarding the salvage tug.

Climbing the gangplank between my two uniformed,

comrades-in-arms I felt more than a trifle self-conscious. For one thing, the motley ship's crew (I could make out some five or six men in all) were leaning over the tug's side, caustically eyeing our arrival, and making several raucous catcalls, obviously directed at me — at my extreme youth, my unblemished complexion, and, of course, at a hoped-for sexual ambiguity. But again I steeled myself against mockery and my presumed complaisance to their every sexual whim, and pretended I was thousands of miles away from their presence and their words of innuendo.

I was very soon to learn that the remarks aimed at me were merely part of a general hostility directed towards all three of us D.E.M.S. ratings, as representing the forces of law and order which were anathema to the ship's company of The Recovery. We scarcely had time to stow our hammocks in the dark and damp of the fo'c's'le (I noticed that where Rice and McBride ordered me to sling my hammock when the time came, was right next to the immense and rusty chain of the anchor which led through the prow to the starboard side of the vessel) when I was summoned by the skipper to the wheelhouse.

He was dressed in a collarless sweatshirt with a general appearance of stain and dirt which, in conjunction with the filthy state of his peaked cap and once-white trousers, rendered a superficial impression of a uniform. He had several days of unkempt growth about his chin and from a distance of several feet I already caught the reek of stale tobacco and drink emanating from him.

"So you're the new piece of extravagance this ship has to put up with. I won't say welcome aboard as I think the whole damn lot of you are a waste of time and money. But here are a few tips that you'd better get straight. When my crew are using the galley — it's out of bounds for Royal Navy personnel. When we're towing, and preparing to tow, I want all you lot below decks. There's little enough room — and none at all for a bunch of amateurs. You have no borrowing privileges with our rations, or anything else. So keep your hands to yourself. And that applies to soap for dobeying your stupid clothes — which you people seem to be doing all the time."

With that frosty counsel I was dismissed from his presence. Making my way for'ard to our cramped quarters, I passed most of the crew. There was no exchange with any of them — or, rather, nothing verbal. I received a more or less hostile glance from each. There was an enormously fat man, swarthy, with scanty, close-curled hair and a mouth of gold teeth which he grinned at me. He, I later learned, was of Egyptian origin, but the rest of them did not differentiate easily. They were all considerably older than me and in fact made both Leading Hand Rice and Able Seaman McBride seem young in comparison. Apart from the Egyptian, who turned out to be the tug's cook, the remainder all had that far-away look of seafaring men, and wore the grimey grease-stained clobber of tugmen. Two of them had sweat-rags round their necks and in those fleeting, first-impressions, it seemed that all of them wore blue-and-red mermaids, tatooed on their weather-browned arms which were exposed to both wind and sun on that April afternoon in 1944.

On that first of my expeditions on The Recovery we spent only the night aboard and never ventured beyond the far reaches of Plymouth Harbour. In fact I rather enjoyed the daylight hours, for as we chugged slowly from the dock to our mooring at the edge of the shipping roads, it was rather like a pleasure-trip aimed to show off the interesting aspects of a great-natural port location, and all the diverse appurtenances of what was then one of the world's largest naval bases.

There were the huge Sunderland flying boats, both riding at anchor and lumbering across the swell for immense distances before becoming airborne. And, of course, a forest of grey warships, with battleships and aircraft carriers riding at anchor; destroyers, corvettes and frigates in long lines abreast in Devonport harbor, and a host of smaller craft from a variety of navies, jammed in the lee of land wherever space afforded. For this was pre-D-Day and part of the invasion armada for the re-conquest of Europe was assembled here. On the green hills of Devon and Cornwall — for the bay divided the English county from the Celtic Duchy — there were numerous gun emplacements heavily, if brightly, camouflaged. From these came the occasional twinkle of sunlight where the afternoon rays fell upon exposed metal. The same was true of the windows of the city of Plymouth and the towns of Devonport, Saltash and Torpoint; the latter boroughs joined to the metropolis by ferry and via the railway link of Isambard Brunel's graceful Victorian bridge.

In fact the whole scene was beautiful that spring day; beautiful and fascinating in the vigour and extent of its wartime activity. I even told myself as we rode the small waves of the harbour mouth, that I was actually observing history-in-the-making, as I sensed and saw the frenzy of preparation for the invasion of that landmass which lay invisible across the waters of the English Channel.

But only cold words came into my head — unaccompanied by the thrill of emotion. At seventeen it is certainly easy to thrill, but the sense of historical participation is uncharacteristic. In this instance, I was certainly no exception from my age-group. So I just leaned there over the prow of our stubby vessel, enjoyed the sundazzling spray, and watched the great world as a delightful pageant for adolescent eyes.

If the afternoon, after the unenthusiastic reception on boarding the Recovery, had turned out to be far more congenial than I had dared hope, the shadows cast by nightfall were more than the lack of sunlight, and grimmer than my worst imaginings! We had eaten our supper of fried eggs and bacon, canned pork and beans, that A.B. McBride had prepared, and we were sitting at the bare table in the feebly lit fo'c'sle (we only had two naked candles to see by) when Leading Seaman Rice was giving me final orders before we all turned in.

"Throw a bucket over the starboard side into the drink, for washing up water, Ops." he told me. "And when you've cleaned up everything down here, for Christ's sake, Bach, make sure everything is safely stowed away," he added in his Welsh lilt.

"You mean they" (meaning the crew of the tug) "might want to steal all our stuff?"

Both of them laughed. "Those bastards?" queried McBride, "They're no better than a bunch of dockyard mateys! They steal all they can at sea from the likes of us, and sell ashore everytime they leave the fuckin' dockyard gates. No, me little Oppo, it's rats. 'Tis bleedin' rats we have to look out for."

"I see," I said, looking nervously about me as if I might at any moment spy the one creature of which I was truly terrified.

"Are — are there a lot of 'em around here?"

"As long as your soddin' arm, some of 'em are. And the funny thing is," continued Able Seaman McBride, "most of the bastards live up here for'ard. Reckon they know what a stingy bunch of bastards those civvies are, up there in the stern."

I shifted uncomfortably on the bench seat, recalling a furry, biting creature running up my trouser leg when standing on a cornmow during threshing time on the farm, back home.

"We ought to have a good fox terrier down here", I said.

"Against K.R. & A.I." said the Killock.

"What the hell's that?" I asked in surprise.

"And you went and finished your basic training, and ready now to serve King and Empire," Rice said — although not in evident anger at my ignorance. "King's Rules and Admiralty Instructions, Bach. The Navy's bleedin' Bible, Boy-o!"

"We brought a wee cat down here once," McBride informed me, "But the poor git took off the minute he saw the size of the rats we got. Wouldna' come aboard again, after that. Used to fuck off fra the hut the minute he saw us getting our gear together."

It wasn't until I'd done all the washing up, and was then unroping my hammock, that the subject of the rats came up again.

"Make sure your footsies are tucked in when you're up there," counseled McBride. "Those fuckers will nibble your toes off, if you're not careful!"

The very thought brought cold sweat to my forehead. I never had taken my socks off in my hammock: now I wondered about leaving my shoes on, too. Leading Seaman Rice swung his lithe body in from the hatch, which was the only means of entry to our quarters. He was wearing only his undershorts and a navy issue singlet, as he'd just been on deck for a pee over the side. As his stockinged foot skillfully brought his already slung hammock closer to him, so that he could slide into it, he looked down at my handiwork on the table. At the neatly stacked box containing the recently washed dishes and cutlery.

"Where's the bread?" he asked.

"What bread?" I wasn't really sure I'd heard him aright.

"Didn't you tell him to put the damn loaf out, Bach?" he asked McBride.

McBride, who was already snuggly tucked into his hammock, cocked his curly head over the edge.

"Too much on me mind Rice," he murmured. "Watching our little Hatter, here, swish his bum around as he cleans up. Makes a man *perverted*, you know! I got something here for my little Bach what's worth more than a bleedin' loaf!"

"You could leave your sewer of a mind out of your own pants, let alone his, Bach," the Welsh N.C.O. murmured reprovingly settling himself inside his blanket. "Anyway, Ops," he said to me, "Get that extra loaf we brought and put it on the table. That'll keep the bastards down there instead of running over us all bloody night!"

I leaped to do as I was told, seeing the ruse to keep the rats away as a blessed relief. I only wished we had brought a dozen such loaves, from the 'purser's' store, where we picked up our rations.

But in the event, the one extra-long loaf did the trick. No rats entered my hammock that night. Only McBride's hand at one point, for a few minutes. In the morning when I awoke, it was not to see shadowy rodents and hear the squeaks which had punctured the long hours of the night, but to discover that the two-foot long rectangular loaf had had each crust neatly shaved off by sharp teeth — and thus reduced to a slender shaft of soft and crustless bread. And by the size of the remnant it was not difficult to guess that, left to their appetites a little longer, the whole of it would have disappeared. I resolved then and there that as long as I slept on The Recovery, no less than *two* extra-long naval loaves would be left down there on the table-top, as bait to keep those rats in the nether part of the ship's scuppers where we were forced to live.

Normally, I suppose, the thought and fear of the rats would have been a constant with me. But normality was neither the world I inhabited in 1944, nor the path I was walking down, during those spring months. Never, before or since, have I been thrown into such close proximity, for example, with the kind of men who composed the crew of The Recovery. Their animosity towards my two shipmates was merely exacerbated, in my case, when, to the spit and polish the Royal Navy exemplified, was added my patent youth and inexperience. This personal disapprobation received lively acceleration on my second or third time out.

So cool was the behavior of the crewmen towards us that Leading Seaman Rice, whose normal attitude towards the merchant seamen was to give them the finger, was constrained to put on a small demonstration to the skipper and his underlings, of the protection our D.E.M.S. unit afforded the salvage tug. It was a grey, heavily-clouded day and the sea was choppy. The feel of that morning, as we sailed sou'southwest out of the mouth of the English Channel towards the open ocean, was of March rather than early May.

The night before, when we had embarked, I had not endeared myself by allowing the frying pan in the galley to catch fire from over-heated fat — which I had vainly attempted to douse by the addition of cold water. The conflagration had been enough to bring the skipper and the immense Egyptian cook running — to curse me for breaking the strict blackout regulations. The tugboat's captain had then burst into his familiar themes of what a stupid little fool I was, of how I endangered the lives of all on board, and was, in any case, typical of the rotten state to which the Navy had sunk by hiring schoolkids and shamelessly putting them in uniform.

Rice and McBride had rescued me from the streams of abuse and almost frogmarched me for'ard and down to our sordid quarters in the anchor locker-room. It was there our killock stated that we would have a demonstration of our gunnery efficiency in the morning, with a mock attack from enemy aircraft, and our retaliation with the strip Lewis gun. He thought it most important that I should play a leading role in these maneuvres, and instructed me carefully as to my duties.

Unfortunately things did not turn out well. When, to the

loud jeers and derisive comments from the assembled ship's company we had mounted the Lewis gun on its emplacement, it rapidly transpired that the first canvas-covered crate of ammunition had been hopelessly corroded by seawater — after months and months, apparently, of being brought on board each time the unit sailed, but never opened. Scenting trouble the minute the tell-tale sight of green showed through the grey-painted box, our N.C.O. immediately whispered to me to quickly fetch another ammunition crate.

In vain. A fruitless descent to our quarters and a frantic search — followed by a hissed discussion between myself and Able Seaman McBride — revealed that both thought the other had brought the remaining canvas bags containing the wooden boxes, and that, in fact, they now stood on the deserted quay where we had left them. That was no time for mutual recrimination, of course, so we quickly repaired to the small space in front of the wheelhouse where we had elected to mount the gun, and informed Leading Hand Rice of the oversight. I saw his face pale, and I trembled at what retribution might follow. But all he did at that particular moment was to seize a crow-bar used by the tug's crew, and attack the ammunition box. When splintered and chipped it finally fell open — to reveal a state of chemical disintegration that not even the green of oxydisation on the outside had prepared us for. I was certainly no ordnance expert but it hardly needed someone from the artificer branch of the Service to realize that what we were beholding had no military capability whatever!

Shamefaced and silent we collected the various bits of our useless equipment carted it once more down the hatchway with us. Once there, however, it was immediately apparent that my two fellow ratings were by no means so prone to treat the matter with excessive seriousness.

"Jesus fucking Christ!" Leading Seaman Rice began, "Trust us to bugger that up, Boys!" He looked at me, actual amusement curling his lips. "You'd better volunteer to help old King Farouk out in his galley tonight, Ops. That's the only way we're going to get back on the right side of that lot. Play up to him, eh? He's number one with 'em. I'll consider that, Bryant, in the line of duty, and not report you to the Jimmy when we get back, o.k.?"

I was in no position to argue: nodded glumly.

"Don't look so fucking chokker, Bash," McBride said to me. "Once we forgot to bring the whole soddin' thing with us. Left the bloody gun behind we did. At least this was only the ammo!"

When dusk fell it was time for me to wander up to the galley and offer the huge Egyptian my services. He listened, or rather continued to slap lumps of liver through mounds of flour as I told him my superior, Leading Seaman Rice, had instructed me to report to him and help out in whatever way he saw fit.

"Boys is pretty pissed off with you," he said, when I was finished. "Better watch your step, Kiddo, or they'll have your knackers for rissoles."

I took the cloth he offered and started to dry the cooking utensils he had washed and left to dry before my arrival.

"We're not volunteers for this job, you know," I informed him. "We're all doing what we were ordered to do."

But that kind of talk didn't seem to have much meaning for the barrel-girthed Egyptian. "I'm just warning you, that's all. There's been more than one of you matelots what never got back to port from The Recovery. Always a bit of a mystery, eh? No one really *saw* nothing. But — well, if a kid's a rookey and don't understand being at sea in an ocean-going tug . . . See what I mean? Like there's hawsers what snap and can cut you in half. I once seen a man's head cut clean off. Then with our shallow draught we pitch a lot and it's easy just to go overboard, see?"

I did. All too readily. Then I did something that just a year earlier I would have conceived impossible — I smiled at him from under lowered lids. The crudest flirtation. "I — I just thought you could give me a tip or two," I said, uncomfortably hearing the coyness in my voice. "The killock ordered me to give you a hand, but then I expect to be going home to our farm soon, and wondered whether you would like me to bring you back some fresh eggs? Or what about some Cornish cream — you ever had that?"

"Come over here," he ordered. "Stand over the sink there."

With reluctance I did so. I didn't care for that expression which revealed his plentiful gold teeth: it was like too many other expressions I had been receiving since my naval days had begun . . .

He took me firmly, but not roughly, by the shoulders of my sailor's broad collar, and maneuvered me until I was standing immediately in front of him. His breath played warm upon my bare neck. In the cramped quarters of the galley it was inevitable that his own large body touched the back of mine. I was acutely aware of that part of him which was pressed slightly against my buttocks. But he didn't try any funny stuff — not that I could have done much about it on that ship, had he decided that that was what he wanted from me rather than fresh farm eggs or Cornish clotted cream.

What he did took me more by surprise — and it was certainly to my ardent relief. He suddenly stuck out an arm, under my armpit and pulled back his grease-stained shirt sleeve to reveal a half dozen or so wristwatches strapped along its length.

"Wanna buy one of these?" he asked, dropping his voice significantly. "You can have any of 'em for fifteen bob. They're worth five quid each at least, on the market. They're Swiss bastards."

I assumed they were stolen. Glancing at them, they all seemed highly ornate.

"I'd love to buy one," I told him. "Mind you, I can't pay right away. I'll have to get the money when we get back to Guz."

That didn't bother him. He was already taking the first one off his hairy forearm. It appeared he had chosen that one for me, and I wasn't disposed to query his taste.

"Maybe your folks 'ud like one, too," he suggested. "You can ask 'em when you get home and are collecting me them eggs and cream. Then I can get you other stuff from time to time. Like cigarette lighters? Real beauts, they are. I'm sure you'll want one of them, Kid."

I sighed, but took heart from the fact that his thighs were pushing less hard against my bottom now. "I certainly will," I told him. "And now, what would you like me to do in the sink here?"

The Egyptian — whom I was soon calling 'Farouk' as his mates did — proved to be the right person, just as Leading Seaman Rice had implied he'd be, by sending me to him in the first place as an offer of amends for the fiasco of our demonstration of the tug's naval protection. On the few times I got weekend shore-leave in the subsequent months, and was able to hitch-hike right across Cornwall to my village home, I always brought Farouk a gift — traditional Cornish delicacies, such as saffron cake, yeast buns, bacon-and-egg pie, and apple pasties, as well as the promised brown eggs and clotted cream. All of it, I may say, most carefully and attractively packed by a loving mother who thought in her innocence that it was for her son's consumption as a relief from, and supplement to his naval rations.

But there was the time, as we rode at anchor on an ink-black night, that I was returning to my messmates, when I was accosted by two of the tugmen who had never directly addressed me before. One of them was no taller than me, but had broad shoulders and arms long enough to make one think of apes. He had thinnish red hair and came from Belfast. He was the scowling component of any cameo of the tug's crew who presented an overtly hostile front to the D.E.M.S.'s contingent on board.

"Here's the little poufta. Been keeping the cook happy as usual?"

His companion nudged him. The other man was a Norwegian and worked usually down in the engine room. Consequently I rarely saw him. He was quite tall, very thin and almost totally bald — though this latter fact was currently concealed by a navy-blue toque which he wore pulled down to his ears.

"Hello, Sailor-boy," he said in his thick-accented English. "You know dat Farouk aint de only one vot likes them Cornish pasties. Why you not bring some of dem for Olaf and Paddy here?"

I could hear the rhythmic slap-slap of the water against our sides. I suddenly felt cold. There was no way to safety, except past the two of them.

"I'll see what I can do," I mumbled. "I must get below decks now, though."

"What's the hurry, Pouf? You done fuck-all for The Recovery. Maybe you can do something else for the two of us, huh? That's why the Navy took the likes of you — not for fighting the bloody war, that's for sure!"

I spoke very quietly. "Can I go now, please?"

"Little shit — you aren't going no place. 'Cept over the side, if you aint careful!"

I had become very still. It was dark, as I've said. I couldn't be sure if there was a knife, now, in his hand. I swallowed hard. I knew I was trapped. Yet in a perverse way, that liberated an anger in me, a violence I had never previously experienced.

"Just let me pass. And — and there's nothing coming your way from our farm, I don't mind telling you that!"

"Oi think this little brown hatter has got to be learned a lesson," the Ulsterman growled. "What shall we do to him, Olaf? The cocky bastard needs to be took down a peg or three, eh?"

The Norwegian towered over me. "Dese bastards don' know who is de *guests* on this boat."

I felt in my pocket for my naval issue, multi-purpose jack-knife. It had a useful weapon in one of its components. Along its spine lay a length of tubular steel ending in a sharp point, known as a marline spike, which was otherwise used for splicing rope. I pulled this open and held the steel down parallel with the serge of my bellbottoms. As the Orangeman's long arm was suddenly raised threateningly in my direction, I lifted my own and stabbed with the cruel spike towards the soft part of flesh, under his elbow. Before any kind of connection, though, there was a bull-like roar from behind my two would-be assailants, and the gigantic hulk of the Egyptian thrust itself across a mound of coiled hemp rope and tarpaulin. Farouk grabbed the heads of both of them.

"Threatening the kiddo, eh? You lousy sods!"

I heard the distinct crack of their skulls in collision, just as they tottered on me, causing my knife to fly from my hands and over the edge of the gunwale into the sea below. Then the burly cook had them falling over one another as they collapsed to the oil-smeared deck. I didn't wait, but jumped over their flailing forms, and in the direction of the for'ard scuppers and the protection of my messmates.

None of the tug's crew actually tried to lay physical hands on me after that. Farouk made his protective role amply clear, and they were all patently afraid of him. But the resentment, the animosity, never let up. And in a way, I sort of welcomed it. It was something I could share with the impervious Leading Seaman Rice and the contemptuous Able Seaman McBride. For the first time since exchanging corded pants on the farm for bellbottoms and becoming DJX 732/367, I felt I *belonged* to something. Only it wasn't to the Royal Navy. It wasn't to D.E.M.S. It was merely to the two of them — in our common detestation of the crew of The Recovery. Although for me, I had to make exception of my defender (and increasingly *demanding* protector) the Egyptian nicknamed Farouk, whose real name I never did learn.

Although The Recovery was referred to as an 'ocean-going' tug, the Egyptian told me it had been built in Greenoch, Scotland, to do tugging duty in the River Mersey and that, apart from its trip around the coast to this Devonport base at the beginning of the war, it had hardly been out of sight of Liverpool's Royal Liver Building!

I soon discovered that it was a rare day when we did not return to the quay by nightfall, or, failing that, would be tied up at a buoy in the harbormouth. By the beginning of June the longest voyage I had taken in her was when we shared with another tug, the task of towing a large wooden edifice which turned out to be an object of gunnery practice for a Free French cruiser now based at Devonport, too.

It had been a brilliant, sun-shot day, with small cumulus clouds scudding a bright blue sky and a glistening sea in the most benevolent of moods, with hardly a swell discernible. We had sailed south past Rame Head and were some ten miles off the east coast of Cornwall when firing practice started. The object of the exercise, it had been explained to me by my fellow-matelots, was to send a first shell over the target, the second to fall short, and a third to bullseye. The target, I may say, was now some half-mile of towrope from our position, and that of our sister tug to the west of us.

Within seconds it was apparent that those Frenchmen had either never learned the rules of that particular game or, failing that, simply couldn't count up to three. There was a huge fountain of water obscuring the other tug with the first shell — in a direction in no way related to the target. The second salvo rocked us and, according to some subsequent accounts, actually sprayed us with water. The third — and mercifully, the final shell — succeeded in severing the rope joining the target to the tug Superior, so that we were left alone with the task of towing the unwieldy wooden target.

We were at that moment, under radio transmitter silence but Leading Hand Rice, who wore a signalman badge below his killock's emblem, was soon returning the flashes emanating from the near invisible French warship, which Able Seaman McBride was taking swiftly down. In seconds we were giving instructions to the skipper to return to Plymouth, towing the target on our own.

The gunnery had lasted only a matter of minutes, but with that cumbersome target to tow, it took a full day of careful sailing for our captain to get The Recovery safely back to port. We never saw that Frenchie again, and the Superior was diverted to activity in Falmouth harbor and didn't turn up alongside us for over a week. Needless to say, there was little else talked of on The Recovery for several days and I have a suspicion that because of my comrades' proficiency with signalling there was a slight change in the crew's attitude towards its D.E.M.S. contingent. In any case, there was the solidifying cement of our common hatred and contempt for those maladroit Frenchmen.

Oddly enough, possibly influenced by the benign climate of that particular day, I had felt no fear. Not even after the first spout of water so close to the ship from the misdirected shell — or in the terse attendance upon the second and third explosions from the erratic guns of the warship. I also had had duties to fulfill as the liaison between our naval unit and the tug's captain — and work of any kind is an anodyne to the apprehensions and tensions of physical danger. This was something that I had yet to learn though, but I did learn it — but by omission, whilst serving on board The Recovery.

Although our schedule varied slightly from day to day, there was a firm routine to our D.E.M.S.'s life on the tug. Dominated by the theme of keeping out of the way of the ship's crew we three simply fed ourselves, kept the rats at bay, polished the Lewis gun, and made sure after the debacle, that the ammunition was both aboard and in tip-top condition.

I, of course, had a few personal preoccupations as well. Not the least of these was to keep that progressively amorous ship's cook at arm's length and, less frequently, the straying hand (to name one appendage only) of Able Seaman McBride of The Gorballs. It was also an ongoing concern to keep on the right side of my N.C.O. Leading Hand Rice was less sexually predatory than randy McBride but he was also a man of much less predictable temperament.

So if I say that life during those weeks and months took on a degree of routine that is in no way to suggest that it became easy. It was then I will only now confess it, that I thoroughly learned what rape was. And let no woman today seek to describe sexual exploitation to me as if I were some ignoramus! At sweet seventeen I was an expert in all these matters of the flesh and the imposition of another's will. I was also beginning to feel that life for me was truly a miserable thing — at best, only to be endured.

Until that soft June night when we rattled up anchor and, contrary to custom, sailed through the murk of dusk for an unknown destination which, rumor had it, was to be the furthest from port since The Recovery had been drafted into war service. It was then I learned of values even more to be cherished than being sexually inviolate.

There was an excitement aboard ship. Farouk in the galley told me shortly after we went on board that the Invasion was just a few days off and that the landings were to be further up the Channel — in Normandy. He said the Germans were intensely suspicious, fully expecting the invasion to take place shortly, but that they expected it to have its main thrust in the region of the Pas de Calais, where the Channel was narrowest. With a laugh and a further exhibition of that gleaming array of gold teeth, he then said: "That's where we got 'em fooled, of course, Kiddo. And we's going to fool 'em further on this here trip of ours."

"In what way?" I asked. "What the hell can an old tub like this do?"

But the ship's cook shook his close gray curls. "'Fraid I can't be tellin' you that. I don't trust everyone on board. You don't want to end up in the fuckin' drink, do you because of careless talk? Be like Dad — keep Mum, as the poster says, eh?" Then he abruptly changed tack. "Remember I'm Dad and you're going to play Mum with me again, all right?"

He reached out suddenly towards me and I noticed a whole new set of watches on his hairy forearm, before I skipped agilely beyond his grasp which had been aimed directly at my genitals.

I tried to divert him from that game and also to solicit more information from him if that were possible.

"How do you know all that, Farouk? Who on earth told you all that stuff?"

But he was put out neither by scepticism nor scorn.

"I got me contacts, young'un. Anyway, you'll see. D-Day's coming up and one day I hopes you'll look back and remember it was the old Gypo what told you — long before it happened. Heh, what about a nice new watch for your old man?"

But my mind was far from his collection of stolen or smuggled goods. The tug had just shuddered and I realized that the engines were racing far more quickly than usual. The slap-slap of the water on each side had quickened tempo, too.

"What's all the speed about?" I asked, not really expecting a reply from Farouk, and conscious of the sudden nervousness colouring my voice.

"Reckon we've got a rendezvous with a convoy. That's the only time this tub puts on any knots. It 'ud be one of them slow convoys, see. And a ship's got torpedoed and is listing real bad. Convoy can't go no slower or they'll all get sunk. That's where we come in. Got to try and haul one of 'em into port. That's if the weather's o.k. Usually means she's carrying some special fuckin' cargo — otherwise they wouldn't bother. With the Invasion coming up they'll need all the supplies they can get, right? So we get to do a bit of salvagin'. That's what we supposed to do all the bloody time — not towing for target practice or buggering around there in the harbour night after night."

"Do you think we'll have to go far out to sea, Farouk?" I asked him.

He wiped sweat from his forehead with the hairy back of his hand. "Depends. Not too far, though. Can't. They call this bastard an ocean-going tug but that's all balls. We've no proper draught. Bob about like a bleedin' cork, that's what we do when it really blows out there. But it ain't the weather what's botherin' me right now, Kiddo."

"What, then?"

"Bloody clouds look like breakin' up. And it's a full, fuckin moon. With a clear sky we're just a sitting target for everything — Jerry planes as well as subs. And all we got for protection is you three arseholes!"

I suddenly felt the galley was insufferably hot. "Thanks for telling me," I muttered. "I'd better let the others know."

Outside on deck I saw at once that the cook's predictions were indeed in process of fulfillment. The heavy black cloud cover had already disintegrated. The full moon shone brilliantly in a wide area of sky and sent a path of moonbeams across the rippling water. The sheer felicity of it was all-pervading and I sighed involuntarily as I drank it in.

I thought I could see a dark shape in the distance and wondered if that was another tug making for the same destination that we were. The Superior, for instance that usually berthed close to us? I walked around the deserted deck which was quivering in the reverberation of the engines below. In every direction, just the endless water — black, where the moon's probe did not reach.

In spite of the noise of the ship's pistons racing it was possible to feel the enormous quiet out there, over the nocturnal sea where no gulls cried. And then I thought of what might lie *under* that undulating surface; of U-boats questing, and the possibility of torpedoes hurtling in our direction, without our knowledge. I even peered over the side, both fore and aft, and to port and starboard, and strove vainly to see if there was any bubbling wake heading towards us.

One of The Recovery's crewmen, a beret pulled tight over his carroty hair (he was another Scotsman like Able Seaman McBride) came round the wheelhouse. I at once felt embarrassed about nursing fears over the dangers of submarines and torpedoes, and scuttled in the opposite direction so that we would not have to exchange words. It was time I joined my messmates, anyway, to learn from them what our plans were. They were sitting at the table in the anchor locker playing cards, as usual.

I told them what Farouk had said, but they seemed quite unperturbed.

"Fuck-all we can do about that, Ops," said Leading Seaman Rice. "A Lewis gun's not much bloody use at night. Anyway there's no Jerry planes patrolling around here. Our blokes are in charge up there. Coastal bleedin' Command and the Navy, too. He was just trying to give you the shits, the bloody Wog!"

"You be careful, Bach," McBride warned me, not for the first time. "That bugger's out for a bit of navy cake and don't you forget it! He'll have you over a barrel and ram you in no time. We've seen him do it with one of their own, haven't we Rice?"

The killock nodded. "You shouldn't be always nattering with him up there in the galley. Got to be a bit aloof, we have. Now I'd better go and see the Skipper and find out what's what. No one is to turn in, understand? Not till I gives the order."

I stiffened immediately. Why couldn't we get into our hammocks, if there was no possible trouble ahead for us? I decided not to stay down there in the stuffy confinement of the locker with its depressing dank and rust-stained bulkheads. I suggested to McBride that he join me above where the air was fresh and you could at least *see*. Rather to my surprise he instantly agreed. A.B. McBride, I had soon learned, was a lover of fuggy atmospheres derived from innumerable cigarettes and considered the activity of dealing a deck of cards as strenuous as any he ever wished to have aboard The Recovery. Oddly, that was not so in our D.E.M.S. hut, back on shore, where he scrubbed and polished with the frenzy of a Dutch housewife. Then he considered that his home, I suppose, and there was neither affection nor respect for the scruffy hole we three were accorded on that old tug.

On deck we sat behind a coiled mount of rope used for hauling, where we were out of the cool breeze off the ocean and, equally important, were invisible from the wheelhouse where the Skipper stood with his senior crew. For a while McBride started out at the panoply of moon and stars and heaving seas — absorbing the poetry of it as I had done earlier, I assumed. That his thoughts were in fact the opposite of poetic, was made clear by his eventual words.

"I hate that fucking sea!" he said slowly. "Three times it nearly done me in."

Rice had told me that his buddy had been torpedoed several times while serving as a D.E.M.S. gunner on a freighter in a convoy. But the A.B. had not spoken much about the incidents himself. At least not to me. Nor did he now, except to say that if he loathed the water (like most sailors he couldn't swim) he hated it even more when the moon was full and a ship was most vulnerable to attack.

"I hope that ole Rice is right and that the Jerries are scared shitless by the R.A.F. Seems to me we're heading towards the Channel Islands — and them bastards has got air bases there, right?"

I was hardly comforted by such reflections, and scanned the cloudless night-sky anxiously. But no planes appeared — then or later. When danger did descend upon us in the course of that long night, it was from a quite different and altogether unexpected quarter.

When Rice had returned from visiting the captain it was with the news that somehow Farouk had gotten hold of the correct information and that we were indeed to rendezvous with the remnants of a slow convoy which had been under heavy U-boat attack for several days, and had suffered badly in result.

We mounted the Lewis gun for'ard, working in the feeble

light but each of us familiar enough with our roles that we could have accomplished them blindfolded. Then, with the gun on the swivel and ammo at the ready, we waited. The crew ignored us as they now huddled in small knots, grumbling at the fact that we would obviously not see Plymouth town that night. The hours dragged by. The tug, rattling and groaning from her straining engines, headed ever westwards. And the moon loomed there, as large as ever.

It was 4 a.m. (I had just looked at the over-priced watch I had bought from Farouk) when we heard the first explosion. We jumped up from where we'd been sitting — but there was nothing to see. Leading Seaman Rice grabbed the Lewis gun and described a 180 degree angle with it. I felt my tensed-up heart was doing just the same. Two more explosions, shorter, more staccato. Then someone shouted to look out from the starboard bow. There, as a faint smudge on the horizon, was an orange light.

"What's that?" I whispered to McBride, ever afraid of revealing ignorance.

"Fuckin ship just bought it, I reckon. That isna gunfire. That's burning. Tanker by the looks on it."

We suddenly altered course, but did not slacken speed. Now we were headed directly for the gradually spreading light. My knees were shaking violently and I felt my mouth was dry enough for my tongue to crack.

"Bring those crates closer, Ops," the killock ordered — and I had to force my limbs into the necessary co-ordination to comply. I could make out what looked like a sister tug headed in the same direction we were. I wondered if there was anyone aboard her who was as afraid as I . . .

It was shortly after that — or so it seemed, for time seemed suddenly to accelerate — that from a virtually empty expanse of ocean we found ourselves surrounded by ships. From his wheelhouse behind our gun emplacement I heard the skipper barking orders, and then a corvette swept across our bow so that we rocked violently from its churning wake. The sky reddened from the burning vessel and from almost the opposite direction there was a yet more violent explosion and a further sheet of flame shot up into the air.

We never did see another warship protecting the convoy although the continuous sound of muffled explosions, McBride informed me, were the sound of depth charges being laid by our navy vessels.

"Convoy's scattering!" Rice called out. "There must be a pack of those U-boat bastards. They only have to come out from their pens at bloody Brest."

There was another bang from the ship we had first seen hit — only this time it wasn't so loud. We were close enough — some two miles away, McBride said — that we could see from the aft super-structure that it was probably an oil tanker. I thought, but couldn't be sure, that I could see black shapes bobbing about in the water. I was about to ask McBride but didn't. I told myself that it would remind him of his own terrible experiences out there — but I knew the truth of it was that I really didn't wish to know if those shapes were human . . .

"We can never tow that," I said — to no one in particular — "the fire will burn our stupid ropes. Anyway, we couldn't get them aboard her."

But we had already veered sharply and were moving away from the stricken ship. The other torpedoed vessel was now all but concealed under a pall of smoke and I thought that might have been deliberate on her captain's part. But McBride pooh-poohed the idea, explaining that U-boats didn't need to see their targets — except through a periscope.

But he hadn't bargained with the commander of this particular one. We seemed to be describing broad but somewhat aimless circles on the circumference of an area in which the two crippled ships lay foundering, when there came the abrupt chatter of gunfire such as I had heard only in training at H.M.S. Glendover.

Then I saw it. The long black shape of the sub, now surfaced, and firing from a gun emplacement on its narrow deck. Things were happening with dizzying rapidity. The vessel whose flames had first caught our attention seemed the object of the German gunfire, for the other ship was by now over half-submerged, her stern stuck up sharply and caught in the moonlight as figures jumped into the sea far below.

I heard our captain scream that there was nothing left to salvage when suddenly a yelling, cursing Leading Hand Rice opened fire at the submarine — although even I realized we were far out of range. But this in turn, brought down the wrath of our skipper.

"What the fuck are you doing? Don't let the bastards know we're here. Stop it! That's an order, do you hear?"

But Rice wasn't hearing anything. Nor, I think, was McBride. They poured their hate, their memories, their frustrations down that swivelling barrel in the direction of the sliding submarine. I was just opening a further crate of ammunition when, from the corner of my eye, I could see that squat, bull-necked captain sending his men forward to stop us. My shivering disappeared. My teeth no longer chattered. They were attacking — and we were the Royal Navy.

"They're coming after us killock!" I shouted to my N.C.O.

I certainly never expected Rice's instant response to my warning. He straightway swung the Lewis gun's aim inwards and fired a burst at the approaching three or four seamen. I saw one clutch his chest and stumble; thought I saw another flung down by the velocity of the stream of bullets at such close range.

And suddenly all was silence. I glanced quickly starboard. No sign of any sinking merchant ship, no sign of the low black outline of an enemy sub. And as for the other tug we had expected to join us for the towing job — no sign of that either. Then was she *there?* I mean, out in the blackness, cut now by only a narrowing silver swathe from a dying moon, there appeared to be nothing. Truth to tell, I can no longer speak with certainty of that other salvage tug, or the merchantmen in the convoy, or even the U-boat . . . .

It is not that memory entirely fails, these thirty years later. I still wear my head of hair, have stayed relatively svelte, and at drunken revellings, can still occasionally know the threat of a menacing male, even behind the moat of middle-age. But I have seen too many movies, wasted too many hours on the endless reels of naval warfare on television, to be sure any more whether the cliched images have not become wedged between tired eyes and surfeited memory.

What does stand stark and etched, however, is the aftermath of that firing spree on our dark and silent little ship. The remaining hands came nervously forward and pulled their two felled mates towards the wheel-house and the galley beyond. We had turned eastward now and the first flush of dawn creased the sky. From the aft end of the tug there came muttering and low talk, but no more shouting, no more commands to us three uniformed sailors.

As a trio we still sat immobile — Rice with his oilskin-clad legs straddling the Lewis gun's mount. McBride sat hard against him, the rifle we sometimes brought aboard gripped firmly in his mittened hands. I sat on an unopened ammo crate and shivered again. But this time from the chill of early morning and not from the fear of death.

There was one strange thing I noticed, though. Rice just sat there, silent, rigid, all the way back to the grey waters of Plymouth harbor. However, McBride talked incessantly — to himself. It was very softly, almost under his breath. I had to strain to fathom his words. They were all about leaving Halifax, Nova Scotia, and some girl there, and then about splashing about in icy cold waters. Over and over again it went. I tried not to hear. I felt that he was reliving something which was not intended for my ears.

When we came in sight of Mount Edgecombe and ahead lay the grey stone facade of Plymouth Hope, I made my way towards the galley again. No one attempted to stop me — neither my mates nor the tugmen. I found Farouk in there as I had hoped. As usual he filled me in quickly on the news. One of the crewmen had a bullet in his arm, the other had been hit in the fleshy part of his thigh. They were both lying in bunks in the cramped crew's quarters and although suffering from a loss of blood were quite comfortable. In Farouk's considered opinion, both would live. He eyed me.

"There'll be more than a sick bay tiffy at the quay when we dock, Kiddo," he said. "There'll be a Master-at-Arms and an escort for those crazy bastards up there in the bows."

"They were only doing their duty," I said sententiously. "To fire at that U-boat was what the Navy put us on board for."

Farouk wiped a moist hand against the close curls of his head.

"What sub, Kid? I never saw no U-boat! If I was you I wouldn't volunteer nothing to no one. Two matelots flipped their lids — they'll spend a month or so in the nuthouse and then be discharged. They've both got excellent records. If you start yacking about subs and things — well, there's no knowing where it could all end. Understand?"

"But the two freighters, or whatever they were . . . and the other tug . . . and why were we out there at all last night?"

"You could apply for a transfer, Kiddo," the big Egyptian said. "Just in time to get you into the invasion p'raps. But in any case, you'd be here on The Recovery until that happened. And you know what I had to do with those two fuckers who wanted to jump you. I thought you was in here with me when those two went off their rockers and started shooting at everyone. Ain't that true? Or was you down in a forward hold?"

I looked hard at him. "Why do you want me to say that?"

He stuck his hands within the thick leather belt stretched tight around his enormous stomach. "Mebbe the Skipper thinks it's best all round. He knows his crew ain't perfect. And those bastards ashore could make life miserable for all of us. That includes you and your pals."

"You don't really think I could let them down, do you?" I said — racialistically thinking that as a Gypo he could quite easily do just that.

"Don't matter what I think. Go and take a look at 'em. They're *gone*, Mate. Flipped. Out of it. They want their ticket, I reckon. Want civvy street again. And there ain't no bastard what can prove they're not balmy if they stick at it. Torpedoed once too often. Swam about there in the oggy till the water got in their ears and they started going out of their minds."

But his last words were addressed to my back as I was already hurrying back to Rice and McBride. "Leading Seaman Rice," I began, "I've got something I have to report." But he sat there as stiffly as ever, his face expressionless, ignoring me totally. I turned to the Able Seaman. "McBride, I can already see them waiting for us at the dock. What the hell am I supposed to do?"

He wasn't about to return to my world, either. Over and over the name Lorna . . . . the cursing of Halifax and some weird talk about not enough daylight and someone named Jack trying to push him off a raft. I tapped him lightly on the shoulder, but he didn't respond to that, anymore than words.

Baffled, frightened, I ran back to the galley a second time that forenoon. Farouk was cleaning up, prior to going ashore I suppose.

"I don't know what to do," I told him. "I don't trust any of you."

"You don't have to, Kiddo. You just bring me more of them fresh eggs from your Rhode Island red pullets when you goes home. And I'll see you're taken care of on the old Recovery. It's still the best bloody number you can work out of them barracks."

I could hear the Skipper giving orders, then the bump as our fenders touched the stone of the quay.

"All right," I said, knowing, that somehow, it was all wrong.

# False
# Start

When I was aged twenty I took the name of Brother Dominic. I took it, I was not given it. I was very ardent in religious matters at that time, both attending the Theological Faculty of King's College in the University of London and working part-time as a lay assistant in a parish of suburban London to help pay my tuition and living expenses as a student. I had also just read an history book about the thirteenth century, my favorite period, I decided, which prominently featured the life of St. Dominic and his creation, the Order of Preachers.

Working in the parish, which was High Anglican, I would have dearly loved to sport the black and white robes of the preaching friars and to have mounted the pulpit and edified an ignorant and Protestantly inclined congregation with the wisdom of St. Thomas Aquinas and Scholasticism generally. But as it was, a timid Rector would only countenance a 'sarum' cassock which, by buttoning at the shoulder rather than down the front, was considered more English than the latter which was regarded as excessively Continental, Popish, or both by such bigots as our boorish and prejudiced churchwardens.

When I sprung the 'Brother Dominic' bit on Father John, my boss, he was a little taken aback.

"But your name is Davey, what's wrong with that?"

"St. David was a dull old Welsh bishop. I want something more exciting. A vision I can live up to."

"You aren't thinking of becoming a monk, are you?" Father John sounded distinctly worried. But whether over the growing return to monasticism in the Church of England or over the fiery idealism of his lay assistant, I was unsure.

I had indeed flirted with such a notion when fancying myself en route to serenity and sanctity and disillusioned with the sordid world, but I did not consider it politic to mention it to my employer at that moment.

"I am worried about the atrocious degree of theological ignorance on the part of our laity," I said sententiously. "And anything which reminds them of the Golden Age of the Preaching Church can only be a good thing."

Father John had offered no rejoinder to this lofty sentiment. I felt a bit sorry for him. He had been ordained after a few years in a theological college but without first gaining a university degree, and then gone straight into the wartime army as a chaplain. I thought he might be suffering something of an inferiority complex. I tried to soften my stance.

"Of course, you've obviously brought them a long way since you came to the parish, Father. It was simply that I thought we might try a few other approaches."

St. Anselm's Rector scratched his long chin. I could see that he was thinking and that sooner or later he would deliver one of his famous pronouncements. It came sooner but it was even more of a *non sequitur* than usual. "How would you like to go to Holland, Brother?"

I could only stare at him. "Er — Holland?"

"In August. With the Young People's Fellowship."

I continued to gape.

"I have connections with the Old Catholic Church of Utrecht from when I was stationed there during the war. You're very gung-ho with all this ecumenical stuff, aren't you? It would broaden the horizons of our youngsters to meet Christians for once who were not English. That should help cut down on their ignorance you were talking about."

I finally got the connection between my remarks and his. I

may say, too, that in those days of the late 1940's, England was an austerity-ridden bore, and my very first opportunity to escape it was certainly welcome.

"I would love to take them," I said energetically to Father Cooper. "And I will delay taking on the new name until I am in foreign parts. Then, when I come home we can start from scratch with 'Brother Dominic' — if that is all right with you?"

The elderly priest stuck his poker amid the dull clinkers of his study fire and encouraged a small flame the action kindled. "You understand the young people today, whereas I don't even pretend to. Whatever you think is best, Davey. I leave it entirely up to you."

That 'leaving up to me' included ALL the arrangements for the transportation of the dozen or more young people who finally signed up for the Dutch expedition, and a checking in each case with parents to ensure permission was being freely given for what was, in every case, the first trip abroad for their offspring. I must perhaps confess that honesty was cunningly blended with vanity when I told all parties that this was also going to be my first trip to The Netherlands while omitting all reference to the fact that it would also be my first landing upon the continent of Europe . . .

On the Feast of St. Peter ad Vincula (August 1st to secularists) fifteen of us from St. Anselm's took over two compartments as the steam train puffed away from the Liverpool Street station platform to the fond farewells and waves of parents, the two churchwardens, and, dressed in a thick black cloak in spite of it being a warm summer's day, Father John Cooper himself.

In my carriage, where I sat by the window in my new cassock bought especially for the trip, were three of the youngest girls: Angela aged fifteen, Miriam aged sixteen and Shirley just turned seventeen; the Hedley twins named Jim and Gerry; Leonard Arliss who was the son of the Vicar's warden, and the youngest male in our party, Derek Melchett, who was severely deaf.

My assistant, Dennis Leathers, had charge of the remaining young people in the adjacent compartment and they were nearly all boys. As the train penetrated deeper into East Anglia heading for the coast, I heard occasional outbursts of cheering and yelling coming from there, and I wondered vaguely whether Dennis, who was a student at Cambridge where he was reading music (he acted as assistant organist for us during the vacations) was quite the right kind of personality to keep his boisterous bunch in reasonable control. But after a while they settled to singing and I was gratified to note that their repertory included such favorites of mine as '*Daily, Daily, Sing The Praises*' and '*The Church's One Foundation*' although they did tend to shout the noble verses of the latter hymn.

That evening, when we had all successfully boarded the ferry at Harwich and were bound for The Hook, I collected them together just before the hour I had decreed as bedtime, in one of the lounges, and, in spite of their embarrassment at being watched by other curious passengers, led them through the night office of Compline with me. I even launched into Plain-song with: '*Keep me as the apple of an eye.*" But they only responded raggedly and unenthusiastically with the required: "*Hide me under the shadow of thy wings.*"

But at least when it was all dispiritedly over they were whispering rather than shouting and the more loutish ones had finally abandoned the irritating practice of throwing things at one another. I decided to utilize the occasion by giving one of my famous 'Brother Davey pep talks.'

"You are on holiday — which comes, let's not forget, from holy-day — and are certainly intended to enjoy yourselves. But very soon you will be in a foreign country and when that happens you won't only be representing St. Anselm's parish and the Catholic religion. You won't only be seen as the Church of England, but as representatives of England herself! If you act like depraved idiots, you won't just be letting me down, but Father Cooper, your parents and families, the Diocese of Chelmsford, the Boroughs of Walthamstow and Wanstead & Woodford (which covered all their domiciles, I estimated) and even King George VI and All The Royal Family. But as I will have custody of your passports and remain in charge of the bulk of your spending money, it will be me who is responsible for packing any of you home on the very next boat train if you act up and betray my trust and affection."

At that I thought I heard one of the girls emit a tiny sob, but it was unfortunately negated by a boyish snigger. So I immediately followed my homily with a quick *Hail Mary* and sent them off to their cabins and bunks.

When only Dennis Leathers was left I suggested he accompany me on a tour around the deck before we two turned in. I had always thought him somewhat shallow with that disdainful drawl of his, but from his contemptuous attitude towards the monastic office of Compline we had just recited, it occurred to me that he was decidedly worldly in spirit. And again I wondered how much an ally and supporter he would prove to be. I was to learn.

The next morning the ride on the corresponding train from The Hook of Holland into Rotterdam was accomplished without undue commotion. True, a rather tearful and moist-nosed individual named Harvey Harris, who sometimes did clumsy duty as altar boy for the main Sunday mass at St. Anselm's, managed to mislay his knapsack on leaving the ship, but the incident was rectified by another boy who saw the object lying on the deck when he belatedly left the vessel after the main party, as a result of a tardy call of nature. Few of my charges, it was to transpire, had established a reliably convenient routine in these natural matters, and schedules were constantly being interrupted by irritating, even *wanton* visits to lavatories.

This may, of course, have had something to do with their general nervousness at a first experience on foreign soil. Certainly, for the initial couple of days, the group seemed somewhat cowed by the gutteral sounds of the Dutch tongue and totally confused by seeing the language written. Indeed, it seemed to me that they obstinately refused to make even the smallest attempt to guess what the nearest English equivalent might be — even when the difference consisted of but a single letter!

Thus, after an exhausting day of sightseeing and a night in a modest hotel in Rotterdam, I had no difficulty in shepherding my flock on to the first leg of our expedition within Holland, which was at times to involve trains, but alternating with canal barges. I should add that at various towns and villages on our carefully planned itinerary, we would be the guests of the priests and parishioners of congregations belonging to The Old Catholic Church which, having broken off Communion with the Holy See, in the seventeenth century as a result of Jansenist influences, had nevertheless retained all the formal ap-purtenances of Catholic Christendom and was thus 'in com-munion' with the Church of England.

However, owing to the frenzied religious animosities that ob-tained in The Netherlands of those times, these Old Catholic churches were usually hidden up alleys and behind buildings that faced the main street. Some of them were actually dis-guised as secular edifices and it was not until inside them that one faced the baroque extravagancies of their historical period.

The first of our contacts with one of these churches was on the Feast of The Finding of St. Stephen the First Martyr, otherwise known as the third of August. On our arrival in the town of Deventer we made immediate enquiries from railway station officials and traffic policemen, as to the whereabouts of the church and parsonage. It did not take me long to learn that, in spite of the recognition of the schismatic group by the Metropolitan See of Canterbury, your average Dutch burgher had never heard of The Old Catholic Church; in fact a bit of a con job had been pulled, I felt, on us unsuspecting Anglicans.

The contingent of young people from St. Anselm's parish was both weary and grumpy by the time we arrived in the bleak parish hall of St. Willibroodis and sat down at trestle tables to plates of sliced Dutch cheese and varieties of rye and other brown breads that were wholly alien to our English eyes.

Fortunately Father Visser, the pastor of this our first host parish, spoke English, and although it appeared that there were few local youngsters to play host to my disgruntled group, the sedate elders who sat on a raised dais and watched us munch, were full of smiles and friendliness.

That situation, however, was to be dispelled with quite un-Anglican dispatch, by Peter Locket, a hitherto quiet youth whose contribution to the social aspects of The Anglican Young People's Association, of which he was reluctant treasurer, had been nil. Whether those quantities of hard cheese owned to aphrodisiacal qualities, or whether he had abruptly decided to mature sexually while abroad, he was the first to leeringly acknowledge the presence of the handful of girls of St. Willibroodis, and shortly after scoffing vast amounts of the food laid out on the trestle tables, could be seen making for a remote corner of the church hall where a young Dutch parishioner soon sat upon his lap and he busied himself with cupping and fingering her somewhat outsized breasts.

It was my assistant, Dennis Leathers, who drew my attention to the matter — but hardly in language I deemed appropriate.

"Young Locket seems to have got off to a good start. I think this trip might really bring him out. He's such a dummy at home. He'll grow up pretty quick, the way he's going. Funny how a bit of foreign language helps. Even when it's only this bloody Dutch that sounds like ducks quacking!"

I seized upon the discourtesy to our hosts rather than Peter Locket's accelerated maturity. "I should be careful what you say, Dennis. Most of these people speak remarkably good English, you know."

He gave me a raised eyebrow and merely walked away. I had the feeling he thought I was being stupidly over-sensitive — or at least stupidly something . . . But I had little time to query my status in my assistant's eyes: not with young Locket so palpably and progressively aroused by the lumpy Dutch maiden squirming on his lap.

Before I had crossed to him, and even before I had decided on what I would say, I was accosted by Father Visser who at once began to put his fluent English to pastoral service.

"Brother Dominic, I must ask you to stop that young animal raping little Elsa van Bijl over there. We Old Catholics do not countenance this kind of thing."

This was the first time I had been addressed by my new name, for I had not introduced myself by it before arriving at Father Visser's parish. It transpired I was not the only one to be conscious of my fresh appelation. Harvey Harris, the mislayer of knapsacks and delayer of disembarkation turned to me, anxiety stretching his less than clean features.

"What's he calling you *that* for? You was Brother Davey when we started out. He must be mixing our lot up with another bunch!"

But there was no time to cope with Harvey's confusion. With my own nerves tightening I rounded on him first. "It's bloody Dominic from now on," I hissed, and strode off in the direction of the amorous adolescents in the far corner. But before I had reached them the couple had become untwined. At least, they had stood up and were making for the back door by the time I could confront them. I was breathing heavily from the exertion of hurrying across the room, but Master Locket chose to interpret my state otherwise.

"Bit hot in here, in'it? Elsa's gonna take me outside for a bit of air. Show me the town."

I eyes him crossly. "We are the guests of these people, Peter, and I don't think Father Visser wishes Elsa to leave just now. In fact he's just told me so."

Plump Elsa rolled delft blue eyes. "He is bloody silly, that Vater Visser. He worry like old vooman. Come on Peter, let us leave these oldies. I shows you where young peoples really like to go, Ja?"

And with that they simply turned their backs upon me and departed the hall. I sighed with exasperation, then calmed down enough to shrug my shoulders. Whatever they got up to, out there in the backstreets of Deventer, at least it would not be the flagrant pawing that had been taking place before the eyes of our first hosts in this country — not to say before the tender sight of my other charges.

The rest of that evening passed without incident, but I could not wait to get back to our hotel to monitor Peter's return and to read him the riot act. To my chagrin I had only just entered the room he shared with a rather sullen youth named Walter Hamilton, when Peter suddenly burst into tears. I had wanted repentance, even mortification, but his sudden hysterical shrieks of remorse were quite unnerving. And to my enquiries as to what was the matter, what had happened when he had been in the company of that obvious little hussy from the Old Catholic Church, I got only shriller cries and more prodigious tears. I could get no sense out of him and it was Walter who eventually explained.

"It was her, see, Brother Davey."

"Dominic," I corrected mechanically. "It's Brother Dominic now."

Walter was a fatalist who was surprised by nothing. "That girl wanted him to get her in trouble, Brother Dominic. He got scared, see. And then they had a punch-up and she called him lots of things he didn't like. These foreigners have sure got the English language off, haven't they, Brother?"

But I was not disposed to chat over alien fluency in our tongue. "Kneel down," I said firmly, addressing them both as I suited my own actions to my words. "We'll have a short prayer before you turn in." I thought rapidly of something I could recite by heart. As a good Anglican I had a total aversion for extempore prayer. *St. Patrick's Breastplate* occurred to me but I discarded it as too lofty for these two. I settled instead on the *Nunc Dimittis* but was straightway distressed to perceive their total unfamiliarity with the words, even though they heard and read them with every Evensong they attended.

Feeling quite unspiritual by the time I reached the '*World Without End. Amen.*' — they didn't even join in the doxology — I twirled my cassock when I got up from my knees, and departed with a hearty slamming of their door.

Before preparing for sleep I sought to recover my spiritual poise and emotional equilibrium by delving into the pages of a new book I had recently acquired in a fit of prayerful ambition. It was called *The Priest's Book of Private Devotion* and contained lots of odd little things such as how to bless a birdbath. But nine-tenths of it was pertinent only to bishops, priests and deacons and I, of course, was none of these. After flitting through its contents I despairingly concluded that its Victorian prudery precluded any advice, intercession, or other form of celestial communication which might prove germane to shepherding pubescent and adolescent English churchpeople in foreign lands and guarding them from the rapacious hands of Old Catholic harlots. I turned for final consolation to the emphatically more worldly ruminations of Norman Douglas' *South Wind* which I had brought with me on the advice of my sage tutor at King's College, as light relief from the anxieties and stresses of tending the youth of St. Anselm's when abroad.

On August 4, my new Saint's Day (being the Feast of St. Dominic himself) I celebrated the event by ordering a split of champagne to share with my assistant, Dennis. Unfortunately, this mild gesture of extravagance was noted by the rest of our party supping at a sidewalk *brasserie* in The Hague, I think it was. They elected to share my new name-day — rejoicing via the consumption of prodigious quantities of beer to which, owing to the laws of England regarding minors, they were distinctly unaccustomed.

I was busily tackling a plate of cold assorted meats, mainly sausage — an economy with which I sought to counterbalance the extravagance of the Moet Chandon — when it gratingly dawned upon me that the party of noisy louts, yelling and dancing in the middle of the road beyond the terrace on which we sat, were, in fact, part of my own 'cure of souls.'

Dropping utensils with a clatter I leaped up from my table and rushed towards them, my cassock flowing open as I had undone the belt when sitting down to sup. By the time I had pushed past several idiotic Dutch waiters — obviously in the pay of my drunken youth group — and almost pushed a table over in my haste to quell these unseemly revels, they had disappeared. I could still hear them yelling at the tops of their voices up one of the narrow streets that led from the main thoroughfare.

Not all, however. The Hedley twins, Jim and Gerry, who must have shared appetites and inability to hold liquor in common with their looks, were puking in unison in the gutter where they were both bent over. I commanded them to rise and return to their rooms. Instead, they sat down on the curb and began to laugh. Or was it to cry?

With their muddied, vomit-specked garments (identical white shirts and khaki shorts and sandals) they were more than

I could bear to look upon, so I turned away, telling myself that Dennis could take care of that dishevelled duo as, by reason of his associations with The University of Cambridge, he would be infinitely more familiar with inebriation and its attendant aspects.

But God, or the malevolent spirit which, I was beginning to believe, held sway instead over this land-filched-from-the-sea, had more horrors in store for me on that evening of St. Dominic's Day. Once returned to my seat and my half-eaten cold-cuts, I found that Dennis had departed in my absence, leaving my champagne glass (in which I could swear I had carefully left a final swig) distinctly empty. I was immediately joined by young Melchett, the deaf lad who was the 'Benjamin' of our party.

Under normal circumstances I would have been glad to have him join me. As he was the youngest male in the group I felt a special responsibility, and his inability to hear things made him especially vulnerable. However, my pleasure was severely mitigated when he plonked a carafe of wine down on the table, filled my glass as well as the one he clutched in his left hand, and then proceeded in his flat voice and slurred consonants to tell me that he was in love with me.

That problem was not in *The Priest's Book of Private Devotion* either. But I was rather more ready for it (owing to some lively and lurid lectures by a professor of Moral Theology at King's College) than either the onslaught of the young Dutch harridan as encountered back in Deventer, or even drunken twins vomiting in the gutters of the Dutch capital.

"You are nothing of the sort," I informed him firmly. "You are merely inflamed by the juice of the grape!" Rhetoric seemed the most appropriate reaction at this juncture.

"I love you," he slobbered. He hiccupped before continuing his nonsense. "You take me to bed, right?"

I discerned a boldness in proportion to his bibulous intake and seized his glass and consumed it in one long draught. But if Derek's voice was slow, his arm was not. From under my nose he took my own glass and quaffed that with one gulp, as skilfully as I had tackled his. Fortunately I had the presence of mind to slide the carafe out of his reach in my direction. That proved, though, to be a forlorn gesture. Tears immediately welled in his eyes and I watched with horror as his lips began to tremble ominously. Peter Locket's lachrymosity, back in the Deventer hotel room had been unsettling enough — but here we were sitting in a public place! Besides, the cherubic-faced youth could have passed for thirteen instead of the almost seventeen years to which he owned. I was in no mind to be arrested for child molesting! "Silly boy! What would your mother say if she heard such things?"

It must be borne in mind that *all* conversation between anyone and young Derek had not only to be in great volume but delivered with enormous clarity and pitched distinction. Already I was aware of a stirring of interest from the other tables — and they were not occupied by members of my parish group. . . .

"She knows, Mum does. She says it's all right. She said she hoped something would happen between us over here in Holland."

I do believe that at that moment I wished I were as deaf as he! I grabbed for some alternate route of conversation. "There's little Angela Fisher. She has a soft spot for you, did you know that?"

"No. And I don't bloody well care! It's you I love!" And with that he reached over and kissed me full on the mouth. I could see that his arms were about to come forward to steady his action by clasping me. I darted back and away with the speed of a serpent's tongue. I also took the carafe of wine, drained the remainder of its contents into the one empty glass, and raised that so quickly to my lips that half of it spilled down my new cassock which, indeed, had already begun to look distinctly grubby. But my goal was achieved, I told myself triumphantly. If he should attempt once again to press his hot young lips to mine they would now encounter the protective barrier of cold glass.

On draining the glass I was still afraid to lower the goblet — until the thought occurred to me that, sitting there all evening, holding an empty wineglass to my lips made me at least as much a spectacle as being bussed by a tipsy and patently overly excited child. I cautiously lowered it, but reared back in my chair at the same time. It was at that moment that my errant assistant, Mr. Leathers, elected to trail once more into my sight-lines. "Where the hell have you been?" I asked in quite un-Dominican fashion. "Can't you see we're having trouble?"

Dennis slid his slim six-foot length into the third chair. "Trouble?" he drawled. "I think it's rather pleasant here. At least there's no stench of ghastly fish and by having embassies all over the place one doesn't have to listen to that dreadful Dutch quacking all the time."

I scowled at him. "They're all pissed," I muttered. "And either vomiting their rings up or behaving as if they've taken a snort of Spanish fly!" Somehow his very smoothness evoked the coarse in me. His interest quickened immediately at my far-fetched supposition.

"Do you really think so? Spanish fly, eh — I wonder where on earth they manage to get hold of it. The embassies, I suppose. Diplomatic bags are probably full of it. Hello, what's up with the little deaf chap, then?"

"He is disturbed by lust," I told Dennis. "And that scowl he is wearing is because he has been frustrated in the execution of his passions. I think you'd better take him up to his room and explain that you cannot necessarily have things in this life, merely because you want them."

A lone tear proceeded to move slowly down Derek Melchett's cheek. I feared the arrival of companions to it.

"Go upstairs with Mr. Leathers," I shouted at the youth. Then glowered at those at neighboring tables who had begun to smirk. When the two of them had departed I made it a point to stay there until all those other busybodies had gone. To pass the time I ordered a further carafe of wine and steadily digested that as I pondered what this expedition to the Netherlands was going to deliver next. But as the wine took effect, the anxieties of custodianship dimmed.

When I finally rose — with a cleverly concealed stagger — the harshness of life had been pleasantly blurred, and I even permitted myself a small chuckle — two or three, in fact — that 'my' youngsters should receive their 'blooding' over drink in their capacity as youthful ambassadors of Ecclesia Anglicana. My new euphoria was sustained when I discovered no signs of St. Anselm's Youth Group, inebriated or otherwise, in the streets of the Dutch capital, and concluded that they had all managed to weave their way to their respective hotel rooms — in whatever condition they were finally in.

At the De Kooning Hotel, along the long corridor which housed all our party, there was only silence and by standing at a couple of doors, I could hear the rhythm of steady breathing by those happily taken in sleep. It was only at Derek Melchett's door, from the room he shared with fat Leonard Arliss, the churchwarden's son, that I heard noises I could in no way associate with slumber. Only half-fearing that Derek was sobbing his heart out in remorse or mortification for his untoward declaration towards me, I lifted my head, straightened shoulders and entered the bedroom to minister to the confused little chap.

The first thing I noticed was that Leonard Arliss' bed, which was closest to the door, was vacant. The next was that there were still two occupants to room 204. The other head sharing a pillow with Derek Melchett belonged to Dennis Leathers.

To say I was merely surprised would be tantamount to lying. I was shocked and temporarily speechless as I groped for words. When they came they tumbled from me in a spew.

"Dennis Leathers, you have betrayed a great trust. You have ignored codes, moral and civil and taken advantage of an innocent. You have perverted a pastoral opportunity and let down Father Cooper whose idea it was to trust you as my assistant. You have consistently flouted and derided those values — Dennis, STOP it, while I'm talking to you!" I could stand that endless writhing between the bed covers before me not a moment longer!

Clutching that child to his breast, like some monstrous Madonna, as he raised himself up and supported his head on his elbow, Dennis finally acknowledged my outraged presence.

"Keep your hair on, old boy. I'm only doing what you suggested at the restaurant. Actually, Derek would have preferred to be in here with you, but I gather you turned the little sweetheart down. So I didn't want to leave him wholly *desolate*. Surely you can appreciate that a bit of kiss and cuddle never hurt man nor beast. Come on Dommy, don't be stuffy about it."

"Stop calling me that ridiculous name," I began, just as he turned from me to re-stroking Derek's blond hair beneath him. "And I don't consider what you two've been up to has been confined to kissing and cuddling. I'm not a complete fool, you know."

"Of course not, Dommy. Sorry — Davey. It's just that. . ."

"It's just that I'm not bloody-well being stuffy but doing my best to keep us all out of prison. Don't you realize that —"

"I think you judge the Dutch a bit harshly, old boy. They're much more civilized about a bit of buggery than our lot."

I tried iciness as a last resort. "May I remind you that the Church of England, as-by-law-established, regards this kind of thing as absolute anathema? What do you think that — that *child*, will make of your seduction of him in later years? You've probably ruined his faith, for one thing!"

"Oh come off it! Derek's been on the game for ages, in Epping Forest, he tells me. And he's only too pleased to have me as a consolation prize since you've repudiated him."

"Where the hell is Leonard Arliss?" I asked, now keen to change the subject. "Thank God he isn't here right now. I wouldn't mind betting that fat little pig's prepared to blackmail the lot of us."

"Oh, he's gone to my room," Dennis informed me blandly. "Said the noise we were making was keeping him awake."

I fled the room. Dennis' *sang froid* was more than I could cope with. I tried to will myself back into the general state of befuddlement I had experienced until entering that room of perverted fornication, and even prayed that the next morning would bring a post-drunken oblivion over the antics of Messers Leathers and Melchett.

It didn't, though. The sights and sounds of those two entwined continued to haunt me. But it didn't really matter any more. For from that time onwards when we largely vacated hotel life for that of the barges along the canals, my erstwhile young Anglicans turned into pagan satyrs with the developing appetites of randy goats. By the end of our second week, when I found I couldn't even round up a couple of them to attend High Mass for the Assumption of The Blessed Virgin Mary, (August 15) I was no longer exclusively worried about the blatant love-making of my assistant with Derek. I was infinitely more concerned about the possible pregnancies of Angela, Miriam and Shirley, all of whom at one time or other, had abandoned bunks on board at night for God-knew-what on shore with either my now uncontrollable young English stallions or tumescent Dutch swains who seemed somehow to have detached themselves from their Old Catholic parishes and joined our party.

In fact that date, August 15, marked the end of our calling upon any more Old Catholics. Apart from catching three rutting Jans and Diks and Hanses with my three most oestruous young ladies, I was also bawled out by an Old Catholic priest for attending a Roman Catholic service to honor Our Lady as it transpired that the minute and unheard-of Dutch denomination with whom we were supposed to make common cause, were full of violent animosity towards the Roman Catholic Church with which I was so eager to see ecumenical re-union. If it was a choice between Utrecht and Rome I had long ago opted for the oldest and largest Christian body.

So it was that evening of The Assumption, while my rebel charges spooned, fawned, and copulated with one another in the environs of the little town of Amersvoort, I sat dejectedly, calendar in hand, not noting churchly feasts to come, but calculating that the following April, around Eastertide, St. Anselm's would experience a rash of births from its girl teenagers. The thought of their little bellies swelling made me very restless. I went to my bunk before it was even dark and willed myself to read The Letters of St. Teresa of Avila before exhaustedly falling asleep.

Sleep did eventually come but it was not to be for the whole of the night. I was abruptly brought to the rude surface of consciousness by the realization that I was not alone on my bunk.

Nor was the alien form which had inserted itself between my sheets there for the pure purpose of sleep. Hands, fingers were foraging about the warm skin of my body.

I scarcely had time to see the long, dark hair of Shirley Harris with her tight little minx mouth, before I leaped from the bunk, all outrage — not to say, prudery. Nor was I consoled by Miss Harris' words of entreaty in the wake of my hasty exit.

"Come on, Dom. I know you've had Miriam, so why not me?"

In the feeble light I could not find my underpants as I'd kicked them negligently to the floor when retreating from the world and its complexities. When I did start pulling them on I lost my balance and fell back towards where that whispering hussy was sitting up, imploring me to return to her side. Her arms were surprisingly strong for a girl of seventeen, as they encircled my waist.

"We all know you've been holding off on the trip — what with all your talk about responsibility and that. But it isn't necessary, Dommy. Really it isn't."

I forced myself from her grasp. Anger now joined my embarrassment. "I don't want sex with *any* of you! Can't you see that? For Christ's sake, why can't you all leave me alone? Just because you filthy-minded swine can think of nothing else!" I could now just see a little in the pre-dawn light. Enough to grab a sock and stand on one foot while I put it on.

"Our little Dominic in his black skirt is upset," Shirley correctly observed, as I leaped into my cassock and yanked on the belt. But there was also an unpleasant sneer discoloring her tone which was not lost upon me.

"You and Angela and Miriam — you three youngest — are nothing but whores! And that's what I shall shortly be telling Father Cooper and the rest of St. Anselm's," I informed her. "Damned if I'm going to take the blame for a bunch of sluts!"

It was almost as if she were ready to parry this verbal abuse. "Oh, we shall all have our little holiday stories to take home with us, don't you worry. F'rinstance, you and that farty Dennis Leathers been up to things, haven't you? And he's been so *obvious* with Derek Melchett — I expect that's been written up in *The News of the World*, even *before* we get home!"

Her words terrified me. I shoved my left foot into the remaining monk's shoe, from under the bed, grabbed both *The Priest's Book of Private Devotion* and Norman Douglas' *South Wind* and stomped out into the cold of the open deck at the middle of the night. Our barge was tethered along the canal. There were bodies lying about even though damp mist hung everywhere. All were motionless — I assumed in sleep. But I wasn't going to hang about for that termagant to appear and start haranguing me in front of all the others. I nervously felt the comfort of my wallet in my cassock pocket, then jumped over the side and onto the towpath. Hobbling the skirts of my robe I began to run along the ridge of the dike.

By sun-up I was boarding the packet boat returning to England. I never learned of the fate of those youngsters whom I fled; I never returned to St. Anselm's. In fact I discarded my new name, and in the same breath abandoned any notion of taking Holy Orders when I was through college. I have to say now that only when drunk have I ever regretted it.

# Connecticut Countess

**M**y initial encounter with Beatrice di Leone was innocuous enough if characteristically odd. I was hiding from life in Altman's store in New York City, standing before an expensive coffee table I coveted but certainly could not afford. Gazing intently, my index finger to my chin, at the oaken oblong, I failed to notice I was no longer alone. I jerked violently when I was suddenly addressed.

"I don't think so, you know. That top looks far too much like the lid of a coffin."

I turned to look at a dark-haired woman I estimated to be in her late forties — which is to say, some twenty years my senior. She was expensively dressed in black and so sophisticated in the impeccability of her make-up that had she been fruit displayed on a stall, the cynical would have been tempted to turn it over to see whether ripeness had degenerated into something less pleasant.

She continued to speak. "When you are buying furniture you have always to visualize the day you are feeling less confident than when shopping at Bernard Altman's." Her accent was superficially British-with-a-lisp, but there was something attractively continental underneath it.

I licked lips, invariably nervous when confronting strangers. "Places like this tend to overwhelm me after a while. I could only feel better looking at that coffee table in my own home." But she had broken the spell of its attraction. Already I could only see the ominous top of a casket in my hitherto prized object. I made to move on. Typically, at that rather irrational stage of my life, I felt a few hundred dollars richer by deciding that I didn't even *like* the table, let alone no longer wishing to possess it.

"I am glad I dissuaded you," the woman said, suddenly closer, and falling into step with me. "How about buying me a coffee as reward?"

I glanced at her, both rapidly calculating whether I had sufficient money on top of my subway fare and also estimating whether in fact she was not a high-class prostitute snaring her prey. But one more look into those merry brown eyes, at the exquisitely applied maquillage and the black lambswool outfit made me feel quite dishonorable for entertaining such a coarse notion. I relented and relaxed. "I'd love to," I told her, thinking even such a mild adventure as taking coffee with a Fifth Avenue matron was superior to wandering aimlessly around with no one to talk to.

Over coffee we traded some basic knowledge of each other. Her name, I learned, was the Countess Beatrice di Leone and she was staying in New York at her brother's apartment on 90th Street at Fifth Avenue, "across from the Church of the Heavenly Rest," she added with a sudden flurry of energy that would have better suited the successful resolution of an argument. Her own house, she then informed me, was in New Haven, Connecticut; quite near that of Thornton Wilder and his sister, she elaborated. Her deceased father, a Polish Count, had been a professor of Philosophy at Yale. Her mother, now elderly, had borne the maiden name of Wadsworth and shared the family home with her. Beatrice's ex-husband, she continued, still lived in Rome, a city she hated and the di Leones, all of whom she detested, including her ex-spouse, were an ancient Roman family, degenerate, dishonest and typical of postwar Italy — a country of which she was patently not fond.

I told Beatrice my name was Davey Bryant, that I was un-married and that I worked for a New York publishing firm. I also told her that I was raised in the Duchy of Cornwall where my father still farmed. What I did *not* tell her was that I had fled England after suffering a nervous breakdown, the genesis of which was an ugly scandal involving myself and another man. Nor did I reveal that, far from being employed by a publisher, since emigrating to the United States, the only job I had man-aged to secure was as an assistant in a bookstore — and that had only lasted for just over a year when I had had a violent altercation with the manager who had falsely accused me of stealing a novel by Joyce Carey and a handsome edition of Redoute's *Book of Roses*. Neither did the occasion seem to war-rant my passing on the information that I was living in a grub-by coldwater flat and that I was nearly broke.

The whole conversation was conducted at a considerable pace, for Beatrice spoke swiftly, firing questions and not waiting overly long for answers. At the first major pause in our exchange she warmed lacquered finger-nails around her coffee cup and beamed at me.

"Good, I'm glad we've done with all that biographical stuff. It's too much like at home when Mother gets it into her head to do her Anglo-Saxon snob thing and forces dinner guests into insufferable conversation about pedigrees. We might just as well be a bunch of race-horse owners discussing breeding pro-grams, I tell her."

I didn't reply. I was still feeding on her exotic aura which stood out so stridently in the overheated and steamy at-mosphere of that plastic coffee shop. I could not get over how dark her nails were varnished: almost purple. The thick, white cup she clasped had a pale brown crack running down it. I noticed, too, how Leone smoked. Neither nervously nor ex-cessively. She handled cigarettes in much the same fashion, I was to subsequently learn, that she approached a variety of things. That is, as if the object in question had just been en-countered for the first time, was mildly alarming, and by a lady should be treated with a degree of detachment. Before lighting up she would hold the cigarette in both hands, rather as a flautist might hold his instrument, and then subsequently keep it at arm's length between puffs.

Before she rose to go she leaned forward across the pink formica tabletop and brought her beautifully modulated features close to my snub nose. "This has been fascinating, Davey Bryant. My best visit to Altman's in ages. Will you come to dinner at my brother's? Next Thursday? At seven o'clock?"

I visualized a swank apartment, a whiff of luxury as extension to her own indubitable chic — and there was nothing that could have appealed more to my twenty-six year old heart. I thanked her warmly and even bent to kiss her hand before we parted, as tribute to the Europeanness of her. The next two days were the acutest frustration as I suffered the hours before taking the subway north to the land of affluence.

But within seconds of the opening of that cream-colored door leading off the amply carpeted corridor, I was enveloped in blissful wellbeing. For one unused to the comfort of attentive domestics, the first such experience can be unsettling, not to say harrowing. But I took to the practise with startling ease. Only the fact of having servants seemingly always in earshot, proved a temporary embarrassment. Not many visits elasped, though, before I was carrying on conversations of extreme intimacy with the fascinating Beatrice and somewhat obscene ones with her monocled brother Hugo and his plump wife, Dorothea — while Lewis, the butler, stood only a few feet away being treated as quite nonexistent by all of us.

I have long ago forgotten the specifics of food but can still glow to the memory of a succession of delicious dinners. Some were intimate, with just the three of them, some large when I was seated next to Beatrice but might be alternatively flanked by an eminent politician, lawyer or author. It was thus through the aegis of Beatrice that I developed a taste for the company of the famous — a most dangerous habit when one is contingent upon others for the provision of the commodity.

Beatrice stayed in New York for a major part of that fall and the truth of it, I swear, is that during those weeks I grew to love her, even if I never wholly levelled with her. I became a regular visitor at the apartment across from Heavenly Rest and facing

Central Park to the west. Occasionally she would invite me for lunch, promising a famous person as bonus if I evinced any resistance. But here my duplicity had to obtrude. While sustaining the pretense of my continuing employment with the publishing house I could not afford to appear too free with my time. So, for lunches at least, I fell to rationing myself to her. And that, in turn, proved corrupting. It did not take me long to realize that playing a little hard to get could pay off quite handsomely. Beatrice was an impatient woman as well as an extremely rich one: a refusal of an invitation often meant I was the recipient of some well-chosen gift at my next appearance. And this in turn spelled a visit to the pawnshop, the certitude of my rent, and an upgrading of the frozen foods that served my lonely suppers back on East Third Street.

I was not entirely contingent upon my friend's largesse, however. By this time my unemployment insurance money had begun, although it necessitated my attending and queuing in a bleak and dispiriting office each week to collect my cheque and to perpetuate the fiction of constant job-searching.

Beatrice was told none of this and I was most careful to drop the odd detail over a manuscript I informed her I was currently editing, or to invent some office anecdote to authenticate my supposed work-background. Fortunately my new friend evinced small interest in my time away from her, but conversely, her brother and sister-in-law were far more inquisitive. In fact, Hugo was constantly ferreting around my background and his wife proved downright obnoxious with her endless questions about my sex-life. For her I had to conjure up a girlfriend back in Cornwall who was to eventually join me, and I also invented a couple of local girls I was seeing and who caused me periodic bouts of conscience in connection with the absent Rosemary, languishing in Falmouth, awaiting my summons and my check for her passage.

This propensity to crossexamine by Hugo and Dorothea Skrebensky eventually attained such proportions that when Beatrice announced it was time for her to return to New Haven and that I would be most welcome there, I was quite relieved. The coarser side of me had already gleaned from the trio that a comparable standard of opulence obtained in the Connecticut mansion, and apart from looking forward to a further enjoyment of an alien standard of living in that quarter, I was also looking forward to seeing Beatrice at a greater distance from Manhattan, where the opportunities of revelation of my fake existence remained a persistent danger. I had already decided that I would not be visiting Hugo and Dorothea after Beatrice had departed. And never did.

If my friends in these latter days, two decades later, will tell you how I quickly grow restless under questioning, I can only add that my fierce distaste of interrogation — however mild and innocent the matter — had a large part of its genesis in that Upper East Side apartment, and at the hands of Bruno and Dorothea.

The other Skrebensky domicile in New Haven proved far more congenial. For one thing I took instantly to the Countess Skrebensky, a diminutive, white-haired woman who kept largely to her quarters but at mealtimes and for aperitifs prior to them, laughed prettily at my witticisms and general attempts to keep the company consisting primarily of younger faculty members, in a jovial frame of mind.

She always treated my well-being with tender concern but without lots of questions, solicitous or otherwise. Indeed, she often seemed to anticipate my moods, my aspirations, and even my anxieties. But although her presence was a warm and comforting one for me, I was to learn that the Countess was no Pollyanna, and did not flee those realities concerning her daughter which might be described as bleak and ugly.

It was on my second weekend visit that she took me aside on the Sunday afternoon and asked me if I would walk with her in the garden before she retired for her quotidian nap. Her snow-white hair had been freshly waved, I noticed, as she took my arm and we passed sedately through the open french windows into the secluded yard with its sumac and maples providing us with a final fall brilliance of reds and yellows against a remote background of cloudless sky. "It is good of you to wrest yourself away from such as Dr. von Blasche and his wife Ethel and all that talk about UnAmerican Activities which you attacked so brilliantly. I'm afraid it must be sadly anti-climactic to detach yourself from their stimulating company for an old lady."

I rapidly tut-tutted such an idea away. "To the contrary, Countess. I can have the company of my peers any old time. It is you and Beatrice who are rewarding to me." Nor was I being entirely dishonest, or seeking merely to flatter. At the most pro-saic — some might say sordid — level, my contemporaries, or those few I had come to know in New York and the handful I had now met from the Yale faculties, were generally incapable of offering me the run of the kind of elegant menage I was cur-rently enjoying in New Haven. And after long months of semi-poverty, that factor stood extra-ordinarily high in my con-sciousness. And beyond such bread-and-butter considerations, I have always nursed a propensity for the companionship of those who have lived longer than I.

But it rapidly transpired that the purpose of my senior hostess' invitation was neither to solace nor praise. I had already observed that the movements of her small limbs and appendages were jerky, that is, birdlike, and I was reminded again of the general impression when she suddenly turned in my direction, the moment we were judged out of earshot of the house behind us. "Beatrice is remarkably fond of you, Mr. Bryant. I presume you are aware of that."

"And I of her," I asserted. "I have never regretted her speak-ing to me that day in Altman's," I added, with considerable understatement.

"Has my daughter ever acted in a bizarre fashion before you?" the old lady asked abruptly. And when I remained silent. "Or ever suggested anything you found embarrassing?"

From somewhere I found the cool to first think and then re-spond. "Not in the least. Beatrice is — well, let's say she's very much your daughter, Madame. She lives by a code of conduct as I'm sure you do."

We had arrived at the sundial with its base of mossed red brick, now littered with leaves. It was impossible to go further for a tall wall completed the garden at this southern aspect of it. We turned in unison, once more to face the imposing facade of the eighteenth century house.

"If Beatrice *were* to say or do something — well, that you considered out of *character*," (it was quite obvious the Countess was picking her words with care), "you would inform me I hope."

I foresaw difficulties ahead. "I'm not given to telling tales," I said gently. "Beatrice is a grown woman. I know that you're her mother but —" I broke off, hoping that she would save me more.

I need not have worried. The Countess merely squeezed my arm in the crook of hers. "Let's change the subject." All the same, I reflected, as we walked, she had conveyed her message and knew that I was unlikely to forget it.

I didn't. But I wasn't minded to recall it until another month or so had elapsed and I was once more visiting New Haven to attend Christmas celebrations with the Skrebenskys, mother and daughter.

On arrival at the train station and deciding to walk the mile or more, I immediately noticed how empty the campus was at that time of year — although on previous occasions I had not been too aware of the university presence, save for the miscellaneous dinner guests when staying at the family home just off the green.

So it was rather paradoxical that during this vacation period I should be made more aware of the student population, for Beatrice and her mother had one as a house-guest. I took an instant dislike to Guido Molinari when Beatrice introduced us before Christmas Eve supper, prior to the departure of all four of us to Midnight Mass. He was olive-skinned, smooth of complexion, and undeniably handsome. During the light, *a quatre* meal, even as I was learning that his family were friends of Beatrice in Rome, and that he was an exchange student, it occurred to me that he could easily have passed for her son. It was an uncongenial reflection.

It transpired that she had not seen him for some years, although they corresponded regularly and he had frequently furnished her with photographs of himself. I also learned that he had spent the previous quarter at Stanford University in California but was to now be her guest until finding a place of his own in New Haven. Here he would pursue his graduate studies in 18th Century English under Doctor Frederick Pottle until the following summer when he would return to Italy and finish his thesis on the Italian influence on Samuel Johnson.

For someone who was steeped in the eighteenth century English world of such as Boswell and Mrs. Thrale, Guido's English wasn't all that good, I thought. But what there was of it grated on me. There was that persistent childish accent that lacked any kind of seriousness although he insisted upon talking about 'Josh' Reynolds, 'Davey' Garrick and others as if they were with us in that room. That affectation in conjunction with the way he positively *fawned* over Beatrice soon set up the sulks in me.

By the time we were ready to leave the house I was directing my remarks and attentions exclusively to the Countess Skrebensky, whilst fervently hoping that Beatrice would be consequently put out. But her little friend seemed to be thoroughly absorbing her attention. Sitting huddled stiffly in the back of the car with the old lady while Beatrice who was driving the Lincoln, chatted merrily away with Guido, I was forced to admit that by now I was thoroughly jealous.

When we returned from St. Mary's we all trooped into the dining room again where Giulietta, the maid, had now laid out an extensive display of cold meats, including a huge tray of steak tartare. There was champagne with which to welcome this secular celebration of the Nativity. It was at this juncture that matters soon came to a head. After just one glass of Moet Chandon and a slice of pate, Beatrice's mother bid us all goodnight. But not before giving me a special hug compared to a cool shake of the hand for Guido. For her daughter she inclined her cheek for the bestowal of the customary kiss, but this she followed with a long, hard glance before turning suddenly and wordlessly departing.

When the three of us were left alone the atmosphere changed rather rapidly. It was no longer my jealous interpretation, I concluded, but a palpable fact that Beatrice was now flirting outrageously with Guido Molinari. They stood side by side at the amply provisioned table, with me opposite them. And she was acting as if the progressively tipsey young man was devoid of arms as she fed his dainty little mouth with edibles of her own choosing. I stolidly munched away at a wing of cold pheasant as they continued to make an exhibition of themselves. And I was not made any happier by my realization of how readily I could visualize my own mother wearing a similar frown of disapproval and framing the identical words on her thin lips.

"Davey, darling, can I have a word with you?" Beatrice said, moving around the table, with a slight totter, I was quick to notice.

"Fire away! I thought you weren't going to speak to me until Twelfth Night or something. Perhaps an old Italian custom?"

But she ignored the sarcasm. "Outside," she said tersely. "Guido, help yourself to more bubbly. There's a Heidsieck unopened in the other ice bucket. Back in a second."

He seemed more than pleased to comply with our hostess' request. Though whether he needed to turn his attention to the further unopened bottle of champagne was another matter. I saw that his brown eyes were now distinctly brighter than when we had returned from church, and the black curls on his head had drooped somewhat over his sweating forehead. He looked a decadent mess, I decided.

Beyond the dining room door Beatrice clutched at my lapels. The champagne smelled sweet upon her breath.

"Well, darling, what do you think of him?"

"Guido? He's all right," I said tonelessly. "Why do you ask?"

"I think we should put him to bed, Honey. He's had enough to drink, don't you think?"

It was on the tip of my tongue to suggest the observation suited her too, but I managed to desist. With him out of the way I would certainly feel more like celebrating Christmas. . . . "How shall we manage?" I asked her, thinking that dragging a reluctant drunk upstairs was hardly to my taste.

But Beatrice was evidently not bothered by such anticipation. "There'll be no problem. I've already talked to him. You'll see."

I followed her back into the room and, sure enough, he

proved most complaisant. There was little difficulty in getting him upstairs, although he did lean rather heavily against my shoulder as we ascended that thick, pile carpeting as it curved up the broad spiral of steps.

At the door of the guest room he had been accorded, Beatrice paused. "You'll get his clothes off, won't you? There's a couple of things I must see to."

The first thing I saw in the bedroom was that the maid had carefully turned down the bedclothes, and that a pile of magazines and new novels had been placed on his bedside table as they were always placed by mine in that house. I also quickly noted that someone had been thoughtful enough — Beatrice surely — to include Italian fare in his selection.

Although he did little to aid me in divesting him of his clothes, Signor Molinari offered nothing of resistance. In fact his face now wore a dreamy smile. He flopped stomach-up on the bed when I pulled off his loafers, and obligingly lifted his legs in unison as I made to yank his navy blue trousers down.

I was wondering whether to leave him thus, clad only in his underwear, when he opened his eyes and called something softly to me. Having failed to catch his words I leaned over his prostrate form and then, to my total astonishment, he reached up quickly, encircled my chest with his arms and, catching me off balance, dragged me down on top of him across the bedclothes.

No evidence from him, now, of the fumbling gestures of intoxication, as I felt his hand grabbing at my belt to undo it. And I grew immediately aware that his body was no longer the relaxed length, under the torpor of all that champagne, but a rapidly tumescing phenomenon seeking to elicit a similar stiffening from me.

Now, the blunt truth of it was (whether I would subsequently lay the blame for such carnal expression upon the quantities of alcohol I myself had imbibed or not) I knew I was about to yield to his passionate entreaties. Then my demeanour underwent a further reversal on hearing a faint click from somewhere behind me. Sexually aroused, stimulated by booze, these things I may well have been — but my faculty for self-preservation was as alive and vigorous as ever!

When I heard that sound, instinct told me it was a door click, that Beatrice was the perpetrator, and that to be caught in a compromising situation with this young Italian would threaten everything between me and my hostess — from genuine friendship to the crudity of a meal-ticket. I leaped to my feet, roughly forcing myself free from his imploring embrace.

I was right. It was Beatrice, there in the doorway, watching intently. As I moved quickly towards her she reached out her hand and extinguished the main lights about the room. There was now just a much fainter light from the side table, controlled from the bed. "I — I don't know what the devil got into him," I expostulated. But the Contessa Beatrice di Leone ignored my protest. Even in that much dimmer light I could see that she was smiling. She reached up with a varnished fingernail and laid it lightly upon my lips.

"Don't let me interrupt the two of you, darling. Go on back. I'll just sit quietly over there. Pretend you're alone."

I wanted to disbelieve my ears, to be convinced that the aplomb contained in her so-conversational tone was false and that at any moment, she would begin to commiserate with me for falling victim to Guido's perverse wiles. But all that was wishful thinking. She even continued. "Go *on*, darling! Go back to him. He's wanted you all evening, didn't you realize?"

"Davee!" The voice from the bed was full of pleading. It was more than I could stand. I was out of that room as fast as I could make it. Beatrice was at my heels.

She caught me up, out there on the first floor. "Where the hell are you going?" I winced at the loudness of her voice, expecting the petite figure of her mother to materialize at any moment.

"I don't think you understand, Beatrice," I began. "I'm obviously not what you think."

She more or less shoved me into the adjoining bedroom, which happened to be her own. Her liquor supply on a table by the window seemed as prodigious as that we had left in the dining room. She didn't speak until she had poured us both a substantial slug of scotch and offered me mine. "Who're we kidding, Davey?"

I knew all right what she meant, but I wasn't going to yield the kind of knowledge about myself that she desired. "I am not kidding anybody, Beatrice. I hope that you're not either."

"One thing is certain, darling. Guido isn't. He's still waiting. You make me almost like Italians. They're animals, but at least they're *honest*."

I refused to respond to the latter taunt. "He'll have to wait until at least next Christmas if it's me he's waiting for. Maybe *you* should comfort him instead, Countess. *Noblesse oblige,* and all that?"

With such an innocent piece of badinage her demeanor changed drastically. "How dare you!"

I backed away until the table laden with bottles stood between us. I had seen Beatrice cross with others, seen her sail suddenly, imperiously, against her brother and sister-in-law when she thought her will was being thwarted. But I had never been the object of her ire. It was not a pleasant experience. Hastily I tried to make amends. "It was only a suggestion. I didn't for a second think you —"

"You should be in there now, where you belong — in bed with him," she hissed. "Don't tell me you're not a queer. I've known it all along. Why, the day we met I thought of Guido there in California, as the perfect solution. I planned everything up to tonight. He's just right for you. He's always been looking for someone brighter, or more sly than he is. He's a bit shy, that's all. But what do you do when I try and put everything together? You play sulky prima-donna when I give you such a magnificent Christmas present! You even continue with your stupid game of pretending to be interested in me."

That stung my eyes to moisture with its unfairness. "I thought we were true friends. That over these past months —"

She no longer bothered to even control the contempt in her voice. "Over these months when you were living off us Skrebenskys most of the time?"

I had a temper too. I threw the contents of my tumbler at her, saw her heavy make-up dissolve in the sluicing scotch. "You little gigolo pouf" she shouted. "Get out of this house and crawl back to your slum and your unemployment."

I think I was about to cross back to her to — well, I was unsure of anything save my anger. But the devastating import of her savage comment stopped me in my tracks. "What the hell do you know about me, you ageing cow! You never listen to anyone. Just keep on with your boring, snobbish remarks about your so-called inferiors. You think you can buy all you need, don't you? Well, I'm no Italian kid who'll fuck like a bunny for a few paltry lira. I'm no Guido! My family, I'll have you know, is as old as yours. Only *we* don't have to keep reminding people."

Then the verbal brawling between us turned into something far more humiliating. Beatrice flung herself at me, biting, scratching, shrieking. The words, the violent abuse, became lost in her frantic pummeling. There was a moment, as I raised my arms, not as adversary, but to defend my eyes from her wicked nails, when I felt I had stepped outside of the whole event. As if from a height, from the ceiling perhaps, I saw the two of us there, shouting and swaying, locked in battle.

"I hate you. I hate men. I hate you all," I heard her hiss in savage spurts as her blows continued against my person. And for myself, extra-terratorially, I saw my response.

"And I hate you. I hate rich women who think they can buy what they want." But I only saw such words frame on my lips. They were unaccompanied by sound. "I will do as you ask, do as you want," I wordlessly told her, "because I do love your manner of life and the soothe of riches. But as I reserve the right to breathe, I reserve the right to hate, too." And still no sound came.

At that moment, though, the bedroom door opened, to allow the Countess Skrebensky to enter. I rapidly returned to my skin. Ignoring me initially, the old lady went straight to her daughter, clawed at her bare shoulders with wrinkled hands, and ordered her away from me. "It is time you went to bed, Beatrice. Now let this young man retire."

In a sort of daze, Beatrice sagged at her mother's voice. Her arms flopped to her sides. "Yes, Mama. I'm sorry, darling. The champagne — all the excitement."

"I quite understand, Beatrice. Now say goodnight."

"Good night," said Beatrice di Leone. Only it was with the voice of a child bidding its parents adieu.

I escorted the Countess Skrebensky outside to the hallway. "I must apologize for Beatrice's behavior," she said firmly. "It cannot have been nice for you. She doesn't often drink as much."

"I've never seen her quite — well, so *disturbed*," I said helpfully. "It must've been the strain of Christmas and all that."

"All that — meaning Guido?" the Countess said. "Did she make any untoward suggestion to you, Davey? You remember our earlier conversation?"

I was remembering aught else, of course. "She asked me to help Guido into bed — he himself was feeling none too well, I gather." Never had I selected words with more care.

The old lady sat down on one of the high-back chairs that ranged at intervals down the hall. "And she came into the guestroom while you were undressing him, I suppose?"

She spoke calmly enough but I knew what was going on in her deeper down. I suddenly admired the old girl very, very much. "I — I must have been taking a long time. He was very drunk, Countess. It was all I could do to keep him in bed."

"She wanted you to — to —" for the first time Countess Skrybensky faltered. "She didn't want to leave, I imagine."

A silence hung between us, heavy, unwieldy. I felt powerless; entirely at the mercy of her courage to continue. Eventually she coughed discreetly. The rope of pearls around her somewhat scraggy neck, moved up and down. It was only then I realized that she had not undressed and gone to bed when she had left us in the dining room. "You are still young. How old were you in the war?"

"In my early teens. Why?"

"Beatrice was a young woman when the Germans occupied Rome. So was Guido's father. They were savage, anarchic times. Something happened." She paused, and in the space I stupidly echoed her.

"Something happened."

She looked at me then as if I were definitely deficient in wits. "He raped her," she explained, each word delivered with the dispassion of ice. "She was herself pregnant at the time. It put an end to that among other things."

"Poor Beatrice," I managed.

"Poor Guido," she supplemented. "When Beatrice found out during their correspondence that he had that thing that men get about other men, she included his kind in her hatred of ordinary men. A way of getting at his father, I suppose."

I assumed she was including me along with Guido. "But Beatrice and I have always got on famously," I said, not wanting to believe otherwise.

"Feigned," her mother announced. "I've always been waiting for what she would do after she had met you and taken you to my son's place. Then, when we learned that Guido was coming here, I grew very uneasy. There've been incidents in the past, of course. Scenes, drunken tantrums — possibly situations in New York or in Europe to which I am not privy. Something like this was therefore inevitable. I am only so sorry that it has involved you, young man."

"I am sorry, too," I replied. And I certainly meant it. For still the thought of Beatrice being insincere with her frequent protestations of affection, hurt deeply.

Soon after that we said goodnight to each other, but once back in my room I paced restlessly from the door to the windows and back again. Finally, I came to a conclusion. When I had judged that the old lady had this time truly retired for the night, I vacated my room and crossed to Beatrice's. I knocked very gently on her door but it evoked no response. I turned the heavy handle, found it unlocked and entered.

· She stood there in the center of the room, staring at me. I said the first words that came into my head. "It's started to snow. We're going to have a white Christmas, after all."

"That's what you've come in here to tell me?"

"No," I replied, hanging my head. "I've come to apologize." She was now wearing a negligee, filmy, 'intensely feminine' in the usage of the time. "I haven't been all that truthful with you, Beatrice. I haven't told you a lot of things about myself."

But even the threat of such knowledge seemed to undo her. She held up her bare arms as if combatting some physical threat and began to run about the room. The material of her nightgown lifted in the vortex of the air-current her movement created. I thought of some gigantic moth fleeing the hot burning from a naked light. "I don't want to know. Forget it, do you hear? It was all a mistake." Her voice, always contralto became even lower. "Let it rest there. Let it rest."

But I was off now on the exhilarating wings of self-confession. "I could have done things with Guido. I lied to you when I said I could not."

She ran to the window and herself watched the snowflakes falling. I could see her shoulders convulsing. "It doesn't *matter*, Davey. Don't torture yourself. Don't torture me."

I was now quite deaf to such entreaties. Her body's shaking, her facial features which I could not see but which I knew were now contorted with tears — it all reached deeply into me. "I know about you, too. Your mother told me about the war, about Guido's father. I can understand all that Beatrice. I know about being hurt and ashamed."

She went quite still after that. Her hands covered her face. The white silence beyond the window panes seemed to enter there with us.

"Let's both get into your bed, Beatrice. Let's comfort one another."

"I can't! I can't!" Her voice curved in a wail.

"Not to do anything," I said quickly. "Just to lie there together. Just the two of us — sharing a wound and a secret." I was only whispering. I don't even know whether she heard me or not. However, she let me approach and embrace her, and lead her across to the bed. Unresisting, she allowed me to help her lie down on the pink softness of her silk bedsheets. Then I crossed at the foot of the enormous bed and on the opposite side, slowly divested myself of my clothes, down to my undergarments. Then I got into bed and pulled the covers over both of us.

Since I had left her side she had turned and faced away so that her back was now confronting me. I placed my hand across her shoulder and my shape fitted snugly into the curve of hers. "We're both a bit of a mess" I told the nape of her neck. "I think that's why we're so close."

She didn't understand — or maybe failed to hear properly. She trembled all over without cease. Only after a long, long while, did she say anything at all. "If you touch me — my skin to yours," she said tremulously, "I'll scream." But I could detect the fatigue in her voice. The protest was almost mechanical.

I didn't answer. Instead I thought of the two of us — rather incongruously in view of the disparity in our ages and background — as two children sent to bed in punishment and joined in a mutual affliction, the nature of which I couldn't make out. And drowsily wondering what it was that made our poor flesh a barrier rather than a conduit between us, I stumbled eventually upon the temporary solution of sleep.

# Who
# Shall Be
# The Judge?

Just one hour before I was to participate in my first American cocktail party my hostess, Eleanor Namath, lectured me as I sat huddled unhappily on the linen-basket at the side of her bathtub in which she lay. I was unhappy because the proximity of the receptacle on which she had commanded me to perch, to her fleshly presence was such that I could not fail to see various parts of her body peep pinkly through the suds.

She was lecturing me precisely because she was crossly aware of my unease over the female form in general and her own slim body in particular. "You must circulate, Davey, and not stop and slobber over the first man who attracts you. And for God's sake steer clear of that limp-wristed affectation I've seen you employ when you're feeling unsure of yourself. These are all sophisticated people and quite aware of your kind of neuroses. Only they don't like a lot of effeminate camp stuffed under their noses."

I saw her left breast, like a submarine's conning tower, semi-surface amid the bubbles, and I almost fell off the linen basket when the undulations of her body momentarily parted the waters and exposed her flat stomach and navel. Terrified that in split seconds the absence of foam would reveal the totality of her below the belly button, I turned my head away.

She at once noticed the action. "Afraid you'll get horny if you see too much of me? It's nothing to be ashamed of you know."

I bit my lip and slowly turned back towards her. My innards sagged in relief as I immediately noted that the waves had subsided and that the surface of her bath tub was once more all safely concealing white foam.

I steeled myself for what I felt prudence demanded I do next — for I knew I wasn't imagining that increasing grate to her voice and with what deliberation she had first raised those bristling dugs and then arched her spine to reveal more and more of her. "Would you like me to suds your back?" I enquired. "Or anywhere else for that matter?"

It was in an acute state of tension that I awaited her response. She, on the other hand, relaxed palpably. "I thought you'd never ask," she said dreamily. "I'll turn over and you can start between my shoulders. Use that sponge over there."

Leadenly I leaned over for the bright yellow object, telling myself that this was but the price for landing a job — any job — which I so desperately needed. Eleanor had already run through the guest-list with me and I therefore knew that there were at least three potentials who might help me get a foothold in publishing, or something along such lines. And I was certainly sick of the endless door-knocking and filling in of forms at employment agencies which had been my primary and painful activity ever since my arrival in New York nearly three months earlier. "Turn over," I said, eyeing my shoes until that particular operation was completed.

Her bottom, which bobbed up now at intervals, was at least less aggressive for my gay sensibilities than her frontal equipment. Even so, I did not breathe easy: I knew that Eleanor wouldn't stop at my merely sudsing her shoulder blades. Sure enough . . . "Now down my spine," she ordered peremptorily. But I had my guardian angel with me in that bathroom, I happily concluded a moment later.

"Eleanor? You home? It's Richard."

Relief flooded over me. Her husband, Richard Namath, was home from his photographic studio where he free-lanced for the glossies when not away on assignment or merely away screwing women.

I at once straightened up and crossed to the door. She didn't seek to detain me. I'm sure she'd told Richard that I was gay but I was equally certain he'd be quite prepared to disbelieve her if he found me bathing his wife.

"I'm here, darling," she called out serenely. "I'll be right with you. Be an angel, will you, and see how Betty's managing with the canapes?"

"Sure thing," came the response on his plangent, baritone voice. And I heard his feet retreat once more down the hallway in the direction of the kitchen and the black maid, Betty.

"I'd better leave, don't you think?" I said.

"Of course," she replied, not bothering to conceal the rasp of her disappointment. "You'd better start getting ready yourself. I'd come in and soap you, too, if there was half a chance. And I'd sure make a more enthusiastic job of it than you have!"

But I knew that with Richard's return there was no chance whatever of that happening, so didn't bother to comment. "'Bye," I said sweetly, and skipped out and down to the guestroom I occupied and its adjacent shower where I scrubbed myself furiously.

Shortly after six p.m., while I was still deciding what tie went best with the blue Oxford button-down shirt that Eleanor had recently bought me at Brooks Bros., I heard someone arrive at our door on the thirtieth floor of that building at 101st Street overlooking the Hudson. By the gurgling commotion that ensued I concluded that the early guest was a woman. I relaxed over my tie choosing. The prospective employers I was to meet were all men, Eleanor had informed me — adding her customary cautions over my mien and behavior.

I deliberately stayed in my room until my watch showed the half-hour, before making my entrance. By now the L-shaped living room contained a dozen or more people. I searched hastily for my hostess to effect the requisite introductions. But before she had detached herself from some painted frump, with blonded hair as lifeless as spun glass, and approached me with uplifted arm and a merry cry, I had already decided which was Adam Seymour, Managing Editor of Cloister Books, Inc. I wasn't being anything of a Sherlock Holmes about it. Eleanor had already informed me that he was very tall and I was staring at a beanstalk giant of something approaching six foot eight. He wore his black hair in a crew-cut (this was 1955 or thereabouts), an expensive three-piece suit of dark flannel and cordovan loafers over grey-black hose. He was also good looking with a mouth that smiled easily and thus often revealed his remarkably white teeth.

Next to him stood a smartly dressed blonde about Eleanor's age — pushing thirty, that is. About the neck of her chic, black cocktail dress lay a single row of pearls. Unfortunately, the pleasant sartorial effect was offset by a profound and permanent scowl which caused her tight little mouth to contrast harshly with the upturned edges of that of her spouse — if such he were.

Before Eleanor arrived and commenced to steer me to this guest and that, I stood there at the circumference of the assembly, attempting to figure out a few more job potentials. But every time I concluded I'd found one, my sight would return to Adam Seymour, and once more I would attempt to size him up. He seemed affable to one and all, but appeared to put more vigour into his converse with women. A 'ladies' man', then? as my father would have described a certain kind of man to whom he felt cool. Possibly, but there was something else that gave me cause to ponder. Perhaps his effusions towards the ladies was just a trifle *forced*? And at an even subtler level, wasn't he just a little too well-dressed?

Eleanor's arrival and subsequent guiding hand, brought me to our introduction and before our fingers made contact, I was confirmed in my impression that Adam Seymour was not all that he obviously pretended. Our eyes had met before our hands, and in that mutual glance went a wealth of knowledge....

A few minutes later we were standing together behind Eleanor's Steinway, where it was both quieter and slightly removed from the bulk of the party. As we verbally sniffed about each other's psyche I noticed that he kept throwing glances in the direction of the basic-black-and-pearls woman whom I now knew to be his wife. When she eventually became the center of a small knot of men, I observed that he visibly relaxed.

His conversation with me grew a degree more intimate. "You say you worked in London until you came to New York — what did you have there, an apartment, or flat rather? And did you live all alone?"

He smelled of a very nice after-shave which was quite new to me. I was convinced it was expensive. "I had a basement bed-sitter off the Bayswater Road. If I'd stayed at the place I was working — they'd promised me a raise — I'd have probably moved into a bigger flat with my friend Larry. He'd been trying to get me to move in with him for ages, but I rather prize my independence. You know how it is." I gave him a long look, with an accompanying grin of the kind, I hoped, which is described as 'boyish.'

His own glance in return was more enigmatic. So were his words. "Yeah, these things are sometimes hard to work out. You can want things which are mutually exclusive. That one can be a bastard, I know very well."

"I suppose I shall soon have to start thinking about getting a place in New York. Eleanor and Richard have been terribly generous, but it isn't quite the same."

"Did you have some special area in mind? If so, maybe I could help you. If there's one thing I do know, it's Manhattan. Christ knows, I've lived in enough parts of it!"

My sight wandered up his length to his face again. "Of course, it will depend how *expensive* it will be. I know nothing really about this city, you see. In any case, I shall have to put first things first — like landing a job."

He wasn't looking away from me so much now. I reckon I had his interest. And not just for chit-chat about lodgings. "What kind of thing did you have in mind?"

I wasn't going to run away from that one. "Publishing," I said emphatically. "I know that it's hard to break into, but that's what I want to do most — it's as simple as that."

"I'm in publishing," he said slowly. "But I guess Eleanor told you that already."

"Not exactly," I prevaricated. "She said there'd be a couple of publishers at her party — but she didn't identify them."

"I'm with Cloister Books — a new paperback outfit. Have you had any kind of experience, Davey?"

I liked the way he used my Christian name. That was the first time he'd done so. "I've read the odd manuscript for a house in London," I told him. "For the Dolphin Press and for a small publisher named Ditherfield Books."

That was all a slight exaggeration. Roger Ditherfield was an old trick of mine: I had read the typescript of his very boring novel and he'd often talked of using a legacy he'd acquired to start his own firm to publish it. As for the Dolphin Press . . . I'd reviewed a slim volume, consisting mainly of photographs of London's canals, for *The North London Enquirer*, which had been published by that press. But Adam Seymour didn't seem interested in pursuing the matter; indeed, he seemed more than content with my vague references.

"Good! Good!" he enthused, his glance meeting mine again. "You might be just what I need."

I modestly lowered lids. "I would very much like the chance to find out," I murmured.

From there on I discerned a fresh flavor to the atmosphere: a distinct tightening of interest on his part as to my life, and perhaps, loves. "You have made many friends here?" he asked next.

"Not really. Eleanor, of course. But that's not what you meant, I suppose."

"No. I guess I was thinking more along the lines of your friend Larry, in London."

"Boyfriends?" I said brightly. "No, I haven't made any as yet. But I was rather hoping that getting a job would expand my social activities."

I suddenly thought I heard his wife's voice through a cleft in the overall chatter, and I think he did, too, for he abruptly shifted emotional gear yet again. (By all these furtive darts and hops of his I was reminded of a squirrel or something scurrying about the bole of a tree.)

"You must perhaps wonder how I met our mutual friend, Eleanor. Richard and I were roommates at Princeton. And when we came to New York we shared a place in the Village until he met the fabulous Eleanor. She's an Esterhazy, you know."

The talk was losing its desired focus for me. "Look, I wonder if you'd mind very much if we sat down. Eleanor's sitting room is just there and she asked me to encourage people to spill over into it. Besides, we can take a look at the Jackson Pollock she's just bought."

He glanced over towards the cocktail huddle with a faint expression of anxiety. "Well, I suppose we *should* circulate . . . I haven't even spoken to Dick yet."

I was in no mood for procrastination. I'd gotten his ear and wanted things sealed and signed before he drifted off into that lot of dummies. "It's just that a little bit of shrapnel in my left leg tends to act up if I stand too long." he looked quite startled at that piece of information. But I held the pause just a little longer before going on to explain. "During the Blitz . . . a nasty old Heinkel unloaded over our house. It got that part of my left leg and I'm afraid, the whole of my grandmother."

"Of course, of course" he muttered, and followed me quite passively as, in the wake of my rapid invention, I headed firmly for Eleanor's sumptuous little bower where there would less likely be distractions.

He sat down next to me on the sofa opposite the wall which held the fiery, impasto'd abstract of Pollock — the only *vigorous* artifact in that soft-lit room. No one else was there, which was as I'd hoped. However, the absence of others and our proximity on the sofa seemed to perversely engender more, not less, unease in him.

"My wife Adele, and I also met here in New York. Although she was originally from Virginia and I from Ohio. Dick in fact, was our Best Man."

I opened my legs slightly and leaned back on the sofa: closed my eyes. "We have two children," he continued. "Tim is eight and Wendy five." I remained motionless and mute. If he had offered next to show me their photographs I think I would have got up, left the room, and searched for prospective employer number two. But he didn't. What he did was to ever so gently brush my knee with his.

My pulse quickened. He was finally emerging from the harbor of his discretion. I was convinced of it when I felt the backs of his fingers, which were clasping his lower thigh, through my grey flannel pants. Of course those long legs of his were more than adequate excuse for our bodies touching on that rather small couch. At this point I also thought I could hear him breathing just a mite more heavily. "Would you like me to come to the office or something?" I enquired softly.

He seized on that. "I can give you some hardback books we are buying and you can have a stab at doing the paperback blurbs for them. Then we could go off to lunch somewhere and perhaps look around for a small apartment for you."

There was now no mistaking that pressure, two inches above my left knee, for any kind of accident. It was urgent. "Excellent," I said dreamily, thinking now not only of the pleasure of potential employment but of other delights which had been forced largely into abeyance since my arrival in New York, and which Adam Seymour could most satisfyingly supply.

I could feel my nether regions stirring in response to that kind of erotic reflection, and suddenly crossed my legs. But he only pressed the harder. It was the kind of reaction, I had learned from experience, came either from the repressed or the sexually naive. In either case it promised a whole sluice of pent-up energy, in the right place at the right moment. Unfortunately, Eleanor's boudoir was wholly inapposite as to both location and timing. "Do you have photographs of your children?" I asked sweetly, as I shifted into a less recumbent position on the sofa, with my objectives secured; "I would just love to see them as I get so homesick for my little brothers back in Cornwall."

It was at the very moment that he reluctantly delved into his smart pigskin wallet to retrieve the snaps of his offspring, that the stout woman with the peroxide-dead hair, accompanied by Eleanor, arrived to do homage before the Jackson Pollock.

Adam Seymour was on his feet in an instant, bowing over the fat lady's hand, and congratulating Eleanor fulsomely for her artistic taste. After that little flurry he turned once more to ignored me, called me 'Bryant' and suggested briskly that I attend him at his office at ten o'clock on the following Monday, to be handed some specimen books on which I might try out my blurb-writing capabilities. Very soon after that he left the three of us before the Pollock and slipped back into the now crowded living room.

I didn't see him again for well over an hour. It was then he approached me, his arm protectively about his wife, and effected an introduction. He was one of those tall men who are stately with their length, rather than ungainly, and looking at 'long' him and 'little' her, the words 'most balanced couple' sprang to mind. It was even hard to recollect that delicious pressure at my knee or some of his more searching questions. . . .

When all the guests were gone Eleanor and I returned to her sitting room for a post-mortem, while Betty started in on the cleaning-up. Husband Richard had left with a rather attractive brunette who might have been Spanish, so black was her hair, so sallow her complexion. He had muttered something about fixing up a photo assignment with her, just as they were slipping out of the front door, and I observed a frown appear about my hostess' brow which did not vanish, even when we were finally sitting alone.

"I must say you're not much of a circulator, Davey. That's really essential at this kind of function. I certainly wouldn't have invited that lush Fred Ainsley, if I hadn't thought you'd have talked to him about a job with La Phare."

"I talked to every woman in the place, Eleanor," I remonstrated. "And the only reason I didn't chat with your Fred Ainsley or that Nick Moldavi is because you warned me off the men. And besides, I'd already landed a job appointment with Adam Seymour. I'm pretty sure that's certain — so I must thank you, my darling."

Eleanor never relented quickly. "I'd hold your certainty off until you've proved you can do what he wants. Don't count chickens, pet."

"It's not chickens he's interested in," I told her gaily. "It's me! You never told me he was gay, you old crafty! Why not? Did you suspect something between him and Richard when they were roommates?"

The frown knitted tighter than ever. "What utter nonsense, Davey! You people are all alike — always claiming men as fellow-queers if they are successful or handsome — or as in Adam's case, both."

"If he's not gay — then we're living in Cincinatti," I said, trying to keep the sullenness from my voice.

"What proof do you have? Did he take you into the bathroom? Or unzip in here before Ella and I arrived?"

"Crudeness doesn't become you, Eleanor," I said, self-restraint dissolving rapidly. "You're no Tallulah. In any case, it's playing havoc with your European accent."

"I don't have to put up with this kind of thing," she said icily. "After all, you *are* our houseguest."

That was a circumstance I had recalled even before her reminder, and I had already decreed a little lip-biting was in order. "I'm sorry, Eleanor. That crack about Richard and Adam was quite uncalled for." I never was one to soft-pedal anything — whether it was sarcasm, anger, or remorse. So I pushed on handsomely in comparable vein. "And of course you're right. I have no proof about Adam being queer. Just a gut instinct. And I guess guts are no more infallible than the Pope. Sure, if you look at it from the heterosexual viewpoint Adam Seymour does have long legs and this sofa is a small one. And I shouldn't have ignored the two other guys — especially as you'd invited them expressly for me. I really am an ungrateful s.o.b. Forgive?"

This, of course, was by no means the first contretemps between us and we both knew the essential rules of the game. After all, I had no money for alternative accommodation and she was still eager enough for my bod and keen enough to convert me from inversion, for us both to keep a retreat and our self-respect intact. So I waited patiently for her to come up with her extended last words on the subject. Nor did I underestimate the prolixity.

"You musn't always think that a tossed off confession is enough to mollify me, Davey," she began. "If a little loving kindness went into the thinking *prior* to your verbal assaults on me, life would be infinitely sweeter. Nor am I too happy about your allegations over Adam — who happens to be Richard's oldest friend and one in whom I, too, have placed an enormous amount of confidence and trust over many, many years."

I mentally calculated those to be around four — at the outside six — but rules were rules, and one golden one was that you never faulted Eleanor's mathematics. I remained as closed as a clam. She, for her part, drew fresh breath.

"I simply cannot let this matter rest with your allegations over his homosexuality — for if it were to prove the case then Richard and I would obviously have to wholly re-think our relationship with the Seymours. For there is no way we can leave poor little Adele out of all this. Think what a grotesque deception she and the children are living under, if what you say is true."

I duly considered that, as she suggested, and did indeed conclude that old Adam had problems. But I still kept my mouth shut, knowing that she was by no means through.

"Of course, I shall not involve you personally — that wouldn't be cricket. No, I shall tackle it in my own way and just draw him out sufficiently to come to my own conclusions. After all, since you've been here I've learned an awful lot about you people, you know that."

I nodded my head in agreement. What had I to lose by denying it? Then Eleanor characteristically switched the subject. Had I heard precisely what Richard had said when leaving with that swarthy girl? The one with the coarse black hair that looked as if it needed washing? Followed by 'didn't I think it rather an odd time of day to be arranging photo assignments?'

I decided that as I might one day, quite soon, be needing Richard's intervention on my behalf, I should offer him my aid behind his back. On my way to the bathroom during the party I was pretty sure I had seen him in the master-bedroom where the bed was strewn with coats, in a quick clinch with the petite gypsy number. However, it was not of such things that I now spoke.

"Miss — Miss Alvarez, I think it was — works as an executive with the Conde Nast Organization. I heard her asking Richard if he'd be interested in a job for Vogue — on castles in

Spain which they could use as fashion backdrops. It was a matter, I think, of his showing immediate enthusiasm, and I believe he wanted to show her similar work he'd done. Didn't he do a series on old Welsh farmhouses for a fashion article once?"

The question was redundant as it had been Eleanor herself who'd told me all about the trip that assignment had provided two years earlier. But I was getting into my stride and rather enjoyed trying to get someone else off the hook for a change. She nodded and rapidly turned the talk to a general denigration of the other cocktail participants. But I suspected that her concurrence with my explanations was a willed rather than a felt thing.

The following Monday I presented myself at Cloister Books and after an unconscionable wait in a book-lined foyer, was ushered across plush carpeting into the presence of its Editor-in-Chief. What a change in demeanor by the man I'd met at the cocktail party only two days before! Not rude, but certainly curt to the point of being peremptory, he indicated a small pile of books on a low table adjoining the chair he'd offered me. It wasn't a question of first names or surnames. He made no reference to either.

"Please take the half dozen titles there. What I'd like is a couple of blurbs for each inside and back covers, and a few liners." I guess by my expression that I betrayed ignorance of what they were. "Liners? Look, you'd better take a few of our paperbacks and study what's on them. Miss Baumgarten will provide you with some samples on leaving."

I sat there, legs emphatically crossed, thinking of something to say. "We shall, of course, pay you for what you do — even if it doesn't quite turn out to be our style."

I managed a thank you; crossed my legs the other way. He stood up, arm outstretched over his huge, bare desk. "We should be getting back to you very shortly after we receive your material. Cloisters already has a reputation for being no slouch in business. I wish I could say that about some of the hardback firms we have to work with."

I, too, was now standing, and was still stumbling with words for at least a vestigial conversation. "I know," I began, "some of them are absolute horrors."

He smiled broadly, displaying those silly teeth. "Goodbye for the present, then. I hope it all works out."

I wanted to remind him of the promised luncheon, of his helping me to find digs in New York, but away from Eleanor's apartment, I hadn't the courage. "Goodbye," I said thickly — and turned my back on him and marched fiercely back over that sea of gold carpet.

He must have used his inter-com because as I made blindly for the elevator, a gray-haired woman wearing bi-focals called out to me to stop. When I did so she handed me a big, stiff envelope which wasn't sealed down. I could see a pile of paper-back books in it. "Thanks," I said, without further eye contact with her, and knew excessive relief on finding an elevator actually at that floor so I could quickly escape.

Back at the apartment on Riverside Drive I found that Eleanor was out and Betty making herself a liverwurst sandwich in the kitchen. I joined her with that and a Budweiser and we talked (or rather she did) about Atlanta, where she'd grown up. I had decided to broach the subject of Adam Seymour with Eleanor immediately she returned from her luncheon appointment, but I did not do so. Somehow I didn't want to know whether he'd smelled a rat as she'd begun to interrogate him. Certainly I knew that she'd be no match for him in such an investigation.

From that day on all was anti-climax or plain disappointment. I sent in my copy to Cloister Books, had the whole lot rejected, albeit politely, and got paid $250.00 which I knew to be generous. I called Adam Seymour once but he never returned the call. Shortly thereafter I got a job with a smart little bookstore on 57th Street at Fifth Avenue and within a month had a tiny one-room apartment of my own, off Third Avenue on the fringe of Yorkville.

I never did break into the New York publishing business but became an author in my own right after I had moved to Vancouver some twenty years back. But my recollection of Adam Seymour doesn't quite stop there. Just a month ago I was back in New York, sitting with a potential new agent who was replacing the one who had retired after representing me for over a decade.

We had been sniffing about each other in the manner that we middle-aged persons resemble our dogs: she wishing to discover whether I was of a literary caliber worth her representing me and me anxious to discover whether she had the expertise and enterprise to promote my interests some three thousand miles from my chosen domicile.

Not surprisingly (for we had been introduced by a woman who was a coeval and who had lived in Manhattan at that time when we were all young) we were able to unearth a number of persons we knew in common. Rather late in the luncheon I brought up the name of Adam Seymour and it was just as her fork quested a succulent slice of chocolate *torte* that she slowly rested her utensil and echoed his name.

"Adam Seymour . . . How odd that you should mention him! It's obvious you've been away from this town for years, Davey, because he not only quit Cloisters but publishing altogether, ages ago. No one knew what the hell had become of him. Until I was up at Cape Cod in 1969. The cliche topic of that year was Chapaquidick but suddenly one evening at a dinner party, Adam's name came up. Apparently he left his wife, Adele, after many years — disappeared from sight — and surfaced as the much older lover of a very sweet, English boy who worked as a clerk at Scribner's bookstore. I haven't a clue what Adam does now but everyone says he is very happy. So it finally paid off for him at least, to come out of the closet."

At that point I knew I had found an agent, if she would have me, but I said nothing. I, who came out — or rather, who was *booted* out of the closet — aged seventeen as a result of being thrown in jail for 'importuning and soliciting' and then having to face society, including my parents, was in no position to make facile judgments over a middle-aged man who had been deprived of such rawness early in life.

# Cousin Petherick
# and
# The Will

"**W**here be goin'?" my Uncle Wesley asked me, looking up from the supper table, his mouth full of pasty, his beefy farmer's hand clutching a yeast bun he was tackling simultaneously.

"Up field," I lied smoothly, my plans well prepared, such questions anticipated. "I want to get Aunty some daffodils from Trewildern meadows."

"Cows isn't let out yet. Work idn't over wi' milkin', you know."

"I'll do it on my way. That was what I intended."

He looked up fully from his plate, lips littered with pastry, his brown eyes hard with disbelief.

"That's loikely, that is! Well, be back afore dark. Ducks wasn't shut up last noight. An' that fox was about. You can shut the fowls up too, when 'ee comes through Wayfield."

I stared at him, trying to keep my face impassive. That was in the opposite direction from the path I *intended* taking — but I had no intention of letting him know that. I think he took the look as a reproach, though.

"I can't do everythin' with your aunt away, you. I got they bloody books to do. She hadn't even entered the egg money or the milk money afore she went into hospital."

Normally I'd have defended her. If an aunt with suspected

cancer needed defending! But that would've taken up time —
and maybe even another row and my being forbidden to leave
the farmhouse at all, except to do his bloody chores.

"Right Uncle Wesley. Soon be back."

And I was off to see my second cousin Petherick, the man I
think my Uncle Wesley despised most in all the world.

Now a bit about Cousin Petherick. . . . Well, to start with,
he was the same age as Uncle Wesley, that's to say in his late
fifties. And he was unmarried. Now as far as my uncle was
concerned, the trouble started right there. Throw in the fact he
owned the farm where we lived, many of the cottages down in
the village, and that he was as ardent a worshipper in our
parish church of St. Endellion as Uncle Wesley was a supporter
of the local Methodist Chapel, and you have more than enough
ingredients to feed Uncle's ready antagonism.

Those were the perpetual constituents of dislike that invariably sparked the hostility that seemed to flare, more often
than not, when each month Cousin Petherick arrived at our
farmhouse porch to collect the rent.

But behind all that were other things: tensions, dark jibes
and jabs locked somewhere in their personal histories, pre-
served in some aspic of hate from long before my birth. It was
this that fascinated me, this that had arisen a few nights earlier
when Petherick had come and old scandals involving unknown
names had reached my ears as I skulked, safely out of sight, in
the back kitchen. It was this, indeed, that took me now, still
abrim with curiosity, to the isolated hamlet of Polquite where
Cousin Petherick lived alone in his comfortable cottage.

He was out in his garden, picking masses of white and purple lilac, as I pushed my bike through his gateway.

"Why, hello Davey. How be 'ee, my 'andsome?"

Cornishism must be met by Cornishism I decided. "Proper,"
I said. "Been wishy weather though, 'avn' 'er?"

"Good for lilacs boy. Come on in and 'elp Oi put it aroun',
will 'ee?"

Cousin Petherick wore a thick grey flannel shirt (he never
wore a tie) and faded blue denims that I secretly thought looked
ridiculous on his huge, fat bottom.

Picking up another bunch he had placed on the freshmowed lawn, I followed him into his double-fronted cottage where a blazing elmwood fire flamed in his sittingroom, sending a flickering glow about the chintz chairs and sofa, and shadowing the creamy walls beyond.

"Thought I'd loight the fire, you. There's a brave ole nip in the air, spring or no spring."

The chat was as innocuous as that as we broke off twigs and surplus leaves and I helped him decide on vases and their disposition about the snug room. Only when we had sat down and Petherick crossed his legs and beamed at me did I start my careful probing.

"You know, when I've finished with school, Cousin Petherick, I think I'll leave Cornwall and go up country. I don't know England at all, you. Where do 'ee think I should go? You spent a lot of time up there in the past, 'aven't you?"

"What about the farm, boy? Thought you was gin be the farmer in the family."

"That can wait. I should see a bit of life afore I bury meself down 'ere, I reckon. You did, didn' 'ee?"

Petherick uncrossed his legs. "Yes, I s'pose. Back before the War, that is. Well, Oi'm all for experience, Davey, you do know that."

I aimed for nonchalance. Now was the time to extract the first piece of information to illumine one of Uncle Wesley's dark digs. "Were — weren't you to Bournemouth, or some such place?"

Petherick's eyes narrowed a little. I thought he sat more stiffly in his chair.

"Who told 'ee that, then?" (It came fairly casually but I wasn't deceived.)

"Oh I don't know. I think it was Aunty. Or maybe you mentioned it yourself sometoime."

"Used to go up there for me holidays. That was years ago, though."

"Why Bournemouth then? Got family there?"

"Nooooo." He gave a funny little smile. "Not exactly. I — I had a friend there. From down here originally, he was. Helped me get a job in a hotel — when jobs was bravun hard to come by. I weren't no more'n one and twenty. Stayed three years, I did. Then I come home when Mother was first poorly. After that, loike I said, I went back jest for holidays."

I looked at my hands — my mind at 90 miles per hour. "What — what happened to your friend, then? I don' think you ever made mention of him before."

Tiny little muscles seemed to be working at the temples of Petherick's fat face: the tip of his tongue ran lizard-like around his lips.

"Bain't nothin' to tell."

"I — I was there — out there in the kitchen — when you was talkin' to Uncle the other night."

"Yes?"

"Well, like I overheard."

"What did 'ee overhear, Davey?"

I felt trapped. For one thing I hadn't really heard anything specific. Just hints and that. And what my imagination had done with the fragments — well there was just no way I could repeat those things. I think I must've reddened to the roots of my hair because Petherick did a strange thing. He got up, came across to me and put his hand on my shoulder. He'd never done that in his life before.

"Tell me what he said, Davey."

Bluff was all I had left.

"Oh you know, about Bournemouth and that. And some name kept coming up. Bill wasn't it? Bill Jago? Would that've been your friend?"

Petherick's hand fell away from me and I sort of felt his size collapsing there in front of me.

"Know what he is? A vile and vicious man! A-bringin' up of things of which he don't know *nothin'* — nor ever did!"

That was safer ground for me. "He's got a spiteful temper Uncle has — you bain't got to tell Oi that!"

Petherick crossed the room, away from me, and seemed to be looking at the row of blue volumes of his world encyclopaedia.

"The trouble with your Uncle Wesley is that he do despise

me and is jealous of me at the same toime. And a man what is jealous of someone he do despise is in some state, you. He'd do *anything* to get at me. Usually it were through your aunt who I count me best friend. But what with poor Muriel down there to the hospital, he had but to fling his hatred in me face."

"He — he was making it all up then? 'Tweren't true about . . . about . . ."

My voice drifted off into the clock-ticking silence of Petherick's parlour. The quiet seemed to amass, like clouds piling up over Roughtor, on the moors, until it was so thick I could hardly believe it would ever be broken again.

My stout cousin kept his back to me as he scanned the two or three rows of books, around where the encyclopaedia lived. "He's getting out a dirty book," I thought. "He's going to give me something to read!"

I clenched my hands on the chair arms and wiggled my left foot. But suddenly he turned away from his two bookshelves emptyhanded, a frown on his face.

"'Ow old are 'ee Davey?"

(As if he didn't know!) "Seventeen come August month. Same age as your niece, Betty, to Boscastle. You always used to call us the twins, remember?"

That was all just words, of course. Inside me disappointment spread like damp. But I kept looking hard at him, my face not telling him anything I hoped.

"You decided whether you'm Church or Chapel then? Can't go to both forever, you."

(What a stupid question! As a matter of fact I'd decided ages before that I didn't believe any of it — but that wasn't for public knowledge. Not in Cornwall it wasn't!)

"Church, of course," I said quickly. "Same as you. I'm always in the choir for evensong, bain't I?"

"Then — then you should have a talk with Father Henton. That's better than up to Zig-Zag Chapel where they bain't got an education to spread between 'em."

I uncrossed my legs. "What you mean? To talk about you? 'Bout what Uncle Wesley were saying?"

That shook him, just as I intended it to. "No. No. No. 'Bout loife. 'Bout yourself. That's what priests is for, you."

"But we were talking about you."

"There idn' nothing to know about me. That's the trouble. Nothing never happened for me. I had no-one to talk to, moind, when I were your age."

"No more have I. That's why I thought —"

"You got friends, bain't 'ee? Down to school?"

"I'd rather talk to you. They haven't lived, you."

"Tidn' jest living, Davey. 'Tis the learnin' what should go with it that do count."

I decided to take just a little risk of revealing myself.

"My friend Wilfrid, down to school. You don't know of 'un. He and I do sometimes talk. Then 'e's bravun sharp, you. He's going up Exeter to college for his teacher training when he's finished to Bodmin."

"I bain't talking 'bout book learnin' so much. I got me encyclopaedia and I reckon I have read half the books the van do bring up from the County library. But there's things they books don't cover. An 'ere I am a livin' witness to it!"

"What kind of things?" I asked, crafty as ever. (Determination should've been my second name. I wasn't a Bryant for nothing!)

"Oh you know . . . there's religion for one thing. A man can't live wi'out that, Davey. Now there's *one* thing Oi've learned."

"All roight. What else?"

But I couldn't break into him.

"You'll learn soon enough."

"That's what I'm trying to do, that's why I come up here this evenin', if you want to know."

That got through, I think. At least, he started to move about the room, not looking at anything really. Just sort of walking toward the corners and coming back in the middle again. "Oi wish your Aunt Muriel weren't down there to Tehiddy. She's a lovely woman, Davey. One day 'ee'll realize that — more'n you can now."

"I'm very fond of Aunty," I said, full of Sunday-school smarm.

"Your uncle's vicious, and 'ee haven't been all he should to

*157*

Muriel. But there's reasons. Way back. There's reasons."

"I don't want to talk about Uncle Wesley," I told him, though goodness knows where I got the nerve. "I want to talk about you and your friend. The one up to Bournemouth."

"Bain't nothin' to tell. 'Ow many toimes 'ave Oi got to tell 'ee that? I'm here to Polquite and he's Upcountry. That's all there is to it."

"Didn' sound that way to me. Not when you and Uncle Wesley was going at it th' other night."

I didn't know his anger was so near. I'd never seen anything fierce touch Cousin Petherick before. His chins quivered, both his hands stuck out from his barrelled girth and shook in jerky little up-and-down movements.

"Gossip," he hissed. "You'm just loike the rest on 'em! Feedin' on made-up lies and viciousness 'bout things you know nothing about nor never will. Now why don' 'ee go home and leave Oi be? Ask your uncle. He'll feed on 'ee wi' what you want to hear, don' 'ee fret!"

I didn't know there were tears in my own eyes until I suddenly couldn't see him properly as he stood there, shaking like an unhappy jelly.

"'Twadn' like that. 'Twadn' loike that at all. I wanted to learn. That's all. I jest wanted to learn."

I must've started to sob because he came up and shook my shoulders. "Stop it, Davey. 'Tidn' no good that. Now hush your sel'."

"Me and that Wilfrid. We —"

"Stop it! I don't want to hear nothin' of it."

"You — you and your friend — did 'ee —? Was you?"

But whatever had sparked in him had now gone away again. "Best leave, Davey," he repeated, only almost a whisper now. "Oi can't 'elp of 'ee. If only 'ee'd realize."

"Why? Why?" I persisted through sobs.

His funny little mouth stopped trembling and his wings went down to his sides. "I got one thing to tell 'ee, Davey. An' when Oi've told on 'ee I don' never want 'ee to come here *alone* again. Understand?"

I nodded my lie.

He had to find spittle for his mouth to launch his next words. "Oi'm 59 come May Day — and you know what I am?" He brought his huge head close to mine. I could see little veins like the Camel Estuary at low tide, along the bones that held up those podgy cheeks. Hairs on 'em too. Tiny ones. And his breath smelt awful. "Oi'm a virgin. I bain't never touched a body — nor none's touched mine. Not — not since I stood out there in the galvanized bath and Mother washed me down as a tiny tacker."

His words just fell out then, on the heavy breathing. "I bain't never seen a man or woman as nature made 'em — 'cept for chillun. An' I bain't never touched the privates of no man or woman save me own."

He leant away from me, got balanced on his feet again. "Now leave me be. Loike I said. Leave Oi please."

Which I did. With no more words: walking quietly out.

*Being the last will and testament of Petherick Bryant.*

*I am writing this in my own hand without Mr. Thody of Trebilcock, Bassett & Thody, seeing it as I don't want any lawyers knowing about my affairs while I'm still living. But I have been told that this will is legal if I get someone else to sign it. Which I have. And I want Mr. Thody to read it here in my living-room at Trewarne where I come to all the decisions that I write down here. I'm writing this will in place of one I've just torn up because Dr. Menhenniot gave me some bad news yesterday. He told me I got Parkinson's disease and because I've read that up in the encyclopaedia and know that my hand shaking may stop me being able to write before too long, I want to get this down before that happens.*

*Everything to be sold up. I am dividing up what I got in tenths, like the Bible says. One-tenth of my estate goes to the heirs of my cousin Elizabeth Barnicott, deceased, and one-tenth to my niece Dorothy Oldroyd to Bodmin. One-tenth of all monies realized to go to my nephew Leslie Trelooe in Falmouth and two-tenths to my second cousin Davey Bryant in Vancouver, Canada.*

*The remainder, that is five-tenths or half my estate, is to go to Jimmy Tehiddy, eldest son of Harry Tehiddy of the parish of Endellion, who used to work for Father. Jimmy is a fine and outstanding young man who has made a good name for himself as footballer and athlete as well as playing for the St. Udy Silver Band and bringing pleasure to many. I have watched young Jimmy grow up and he has been a great consolation to me in my recent years. He don't know nothing of this will but I know that as an upright Christian boy he will be a marvellous steward of this world's goods in the eyes of the Lord. I do truly love him and know he has the gift of love himself which he has truly shared with me. He took loneliness away from me, which is more than I can say for others.*

*Given by my hand on this first of May, 1960, in my seventy-first year.*

*(signed) Petherick Bryant*

Our coastal sun is rarely fierce in British Columbia, but it can still bemuse. When it pushes away our panoply of cloud, bleaches our log-strewn strands, and blues our sea, it holds us easily in its thrall.

With such a sun on such a beach on Galiano Island, I lay in the summer of '71, dreamily watching the foaming ferry chug through the shadows of Active Pass. Gulls screamed and swooped about her bubbly wake. The sharp trumpet of her echoing horn followed by the steady throb of her engines were the only mechanical sounds to filter through the swish of surf to reach my ears.

I was thinking of nothing — a great Gulf Island occupation — when I heard a girl's voice calling my name. I didn't have to turn to recognize who it was. Only Tessa sounded like that. The funny little rasp in her throat: part nervousness, part vocal chords. And part, I sometimes suspected, part polished device to go with the elfin image suggested by her small body and wide, wide eyes under the cascading black hair.

"I'm here, Tessa. Below the arbutus."

The rustle of leaves meant she was pushing through the red sinews of the arbutus bush. Then my sight travelled up the tanned bare legs, avoided looking underneath the peasant skirt, and met the enormous grey eyes that blinked in the sand-dazzling sunlight.

"What a place! You always find nice nests." She sank down next to me. "Here, this came for you. Ken forwarded it. I guess he thought you were staying at the cottage with me and not at the resort."

She made no effort to hide the reproach in that, but I refused to hear the plaint. Concentrated instead on the pale blue envelope held in her hand.

"Can I have it then?"

"Sure. I wouldn't have dared invade your retreat without a proper excuse."

I knew she was watching me with sweeping glances as I eyed the British stamp with excessive care and tried to decipher the smudged postmark. I probably pursed my lips in awareness of her sitting there, legs crossed in pixie pose.

"It's from Cornwall," I said.

"I know. You told me that's where Bodmin is. And I worked out the postmark. At least the BOD —"

The words "quizzy bitch" flitted through my head as I tore the letter open — making rather a hash of the envelope as I did so. Then I forgot Tessa and her needs as I read the rounded script of Uncle Harry Oldroyd, my Aunt Dorothy's husband.

Botawn Farm
St. Breward
Nr. Bodmin, Cornwall

Dear Davey:

By now you will have received a copy of Petherick's will from Mr. Thody. [I looked quickly across at my leather purse in which that precious document lay folded, along with two other letters from Cornwall I'd received in the past week, but back to Uncle Harry.]

You have probably heard from various members of the family but your Aunty Dorothy wanted me to write before we appeal that ridiculous will as I was there at Petherick's deathbed and know exactly what state he was in. And as member of family by marriage only and with my personal experience on the magistrates' bench, what I have to say will have special weight in a court of law. The death wasn't very pleasant,

Davey. Apart from the Parkinson's desease, which as you know, he had for years, he had cancer of the bowel, too, before the end. I heard him say at least three times, while he was in the nursing home in St. Austell, that he ought to make a will. He had obviously forgotten that silly bit of paper that benefited that crook Tehiddy and which was produced after Petherick had passed on.

I should tell you, too, that Tehiddy never once come to the nursing home. As your Aunty says, he was probably too busy going through Petherick's effects in the house, because all the womenfolk in the family discovered that there wasn't a bit of your Great-aunt Hetty's jewelry left. Not a trinket. And all the things she had promised your Aunty Dorothy before she died. . . . In fact the poor woman must be turning in her grave, to think of those strangers prowling through her house and thieving her things.

Your Cousin Jane, who has been poorly for so long, and who wasn't even mentioned in that illegal will, is now off her head in grief. You know what a favourite of Great-aunt Hetty's *she* was. Your Aunty Dorothy particularly wants me to say we do not begrudge your being left the two-tenths — especially as Petherick was so fond of your dear aunt. But we would appreciate a letter — send it to Mr. Thody — saying you are in agreement with all the family that it is an illegal will and that Petherick would have been the last person in the world to leave what is rightfully ours to a complete stranger.

Yours in sorrow,

Uncle Harry

P.S. Are you thinking of coming over? That would be best, believe me.

"Are you coming up to the cottage for lunch?" Tessa asks. "I want to show you a new walk I've found through the woods."

"Pass me my bag please, will you?" I make the request as polite as possible, considering I'm ignoring her question.

She does as I ask and I take out the other two letters and the will, deliberately smooth out their creases, lean back on the silver sand and hold up the letters to blot out the sun. I start re-reading them. The first is from the Reverend Trewin, an elderly clergyman, vicar of our parish after I had emigrated to Canada, and the last priest Petherick had known.


Dear Mr. Bryant:

Your cousin's will has come to my notice and your cousin Leslie Trelooe, whose sight is failing, has asked me to write, enlisting my sympathy in protest against the outrageous terms. On my own behalf I want also to declare that in the thirteen years I knew your cousin as his parish priest I was wholly unaware of the gross perversion he nourished in his breast.

I am an old man, in my eighty-third year, and as one whose ministry has encompassed many decades, I can only say I was not only shocked by the discovery of Petherick Bryant's secret vice but would have reported him to the authorities (whichever relevant in these corrupt, permissive times) had I become aware of his abomination.

I am sure that as a blood relative you are properly aghast, sir, at this blatant attempt to misdirect family fortunes, but equally as a Christian man (I recall your presence many years ago at St. Endellion Church) you must be revolted by the discovery of a pervert within the sacred confines of family.

Thus apart from gladly acquiescing in your Cousin Leslie's request to support the family in its claim, I would also like to accord you, sir, every sympathy in the revelation of a man given over to unnatural conduct and who once, in the wiles of his hypocrisy, had the gall to suggest himself as my church-warden.

If there is anything specific you care from me, please do not hesitate to write.

Yours truly,

Desmond Trewin, parish priest (retired)

The other letter was briefer.

Dear Mr. Bryant:

I am sure you have heard — or will — from most of your relatives about ole Ped's will. It comes as a surprise to me and the Missus as I really bain't seed much of the ole chap these past years. But we had some fine ole talks in the past and I knowed all along that in his funny way, he was bravun fond of yours truly.

What none of *they* do know is that he has been paying for our Sunday joint of meat, when Mr. Chapman of St. Udy come round with his butcher's van, every week since me and Shirley was married. That's eleven years come Michaelmas.

The money will come in real handy as I would like to farm for meself and not for Mr. Buse. And we have five youngsters here who cost a pretty ole packet as you can imagine.

Do drop in if you ever come by this way and can tear yourself away from Canada where I hear 'tis proper cold. And I am glad you got the two-tenths as ole Ped always talked nice about you. Which he never did about any of they.

Yours very truly.

James Tehiddy


"Anything the matter?" asks Tessa.

Or did she? It wasn't her I heard. Only the sighing wind through the telephone wires on the road from Pendoggett to Polzeath and the mewing of blunt-winged buzzards as they soared above heathery cliffs.

My inner eye saw the soft grey of the granite in that Norman nave where Petherick lowered his large body to the hard wooden kneeler to pray. My nose caught the yeasty tang of bottled-up centuries in St. Endellion Church and found it mixed with the damp and paraffin scent of the oil-lamp cottage where Petherick sat growing old without anyone to care. And ridiculous, sentimental me suddenly wanted to cry.

"I wish you'd tell me all about it, Davey. It's over a week

now. That's why you came over from Vancouver, isn't it?"

That brought me back. I blinked hard and forced a grin. "It's nothing sweety. Really. A kind of joke."

"Funny kind of joke. I called Ken, you know. He told me that someone had died. One of your folks in Cornwall."

"Ken should keep his fucking mouth shut."

"You and Ken fallen out, is that it?"

Ken and me . . . fallen out. . . . Why can't Tessa keep her hopes to herself? Poor old Petherick . . . having spent a lifetime hiding his right hand from his left, now sending his jackal family howling, even as his carcass starts its quiet rot under the trees of Endellion churchyard, where they'd planted him.

I looked beyond her anxious face, avoided the sun, and stared for relief into the unblemished blue. They weren't buzzards up there. They were eagles, loftily sailing. Then this wasn't Cornwall. This was Canada.

"Davey, where *are* you? I wish to hell I could be there with you!"

A last, longing look at the clear, clean mountains over Vancouver Island, an awareness of arbutus and salmonberry tangled somewhere behind my back. Then the downward descent to rendezvous with those kind and large gray eyes.

"Hi sweetheart! Like to answer a couple of questions?"

"Of course, Davey. You know, I'd do anything . . ."

"Here they are then. How much is one where one *is*? And how much is one where one *was*?"

Then I settled back, my hair in the sand, drawing up my knees and closing my eyes, to await her dear, ridiculous answers to such vain questions.

# Closeted

It was the kind of late February afternoon that can send Vancouverites mad with boasting. The temperature had been up in the high teens for nearly two weeks, with the bonus of an accompanying sun and cloud-enlivened skies. The rhythms of spring had thus settled upon us, with the early multi-colors of the bulbs, the hyacinths and crocuses, already pushed out of the way, mainly by the yellows from daffodils, forsythia, laburnum and broom. It was, in fact, the time of our west coast joy and complacency when we become buoyantly introverted in the face of grim weather bulletins still persisting from beyond the mountains to the east.

I parked the Peugeot outside the tennis courts where several young couples were playing — and paused to enjoy the exposed flesh before attending to my own business in the building opposite. There was one pair in particular which held my attention. The girl was wearing a shirt and shorts. The boy was naked to the waist. Neither of them could have been a day over eighteen.

I didn't exactly sigh over the allure of youth — I wasn't feeling *that* old — but the gap of roughly twenty years between us was certainly sufficient to prompt a stab of nostalgia for that energy and freedom from wrinkle or blemish which adolescence can sometimes so beautifully demonstrate.

When I finally turned away to attend to my concerns, it was with a welcome sense of satisfaction. The sun, the bright-colored camelias, the young exposed skin, all melded into a major constituent of the euphoria which enveloped me as I crossed the street into the sharp shadows from the lofty portals of the senior citizens' residence where I had come to read.

I had no sooner entered that antiseptic-smelling hallway milling with white-coated women, looking so briskly purposeful, than the world of color and young life I had just vacated became something of a desperate counterpoint to my suddenly failing spirits. It was always the same. Buoyed by the belief I was doing something worthwhile in reading a story or part of a novel to whichever group of old people requested it, I would forget the previous experience of a Senior Citizens' Home — either private or run by the city — and suppress the unwelcome recollection of stale urine, the savage impact of age represented in calloused flesh, bent backs and skinny arms and legs. In answering the phone request to read for a brief while in this facility or that, I refused to think of the caustic waves of the years, smothering wits, feeding the ache of arthritis, blotting out sight; the harvest from strokes in distorted voices and crippled gait. And above all, the loneliness of those who had lived on after their loved-ones and friends, and now shared the remnant of years with total strangers.

But it came to me, as I followed Miss Moberly, the Social Events Director at Grassmere Long Term Care Facility, to where she had deposited her circle of ancients, just how frail and frightened I was over the geriatric horrors surrounding me. Involuntary droolings from worn-out orifices merged obscenely with the tang of disinfectant; and the sound of a crone crying as she waited vainly for a visitor — these monstrous icons of age depressed the hell out of me.

There was certainly no sense of moral smugness in me at this example in good works. Only a glum acceptance of my selfish inability to cope with it all. When I had first agreed to give a reading before an old people's group I had mentioned it to several friends, particularly fellow-writers, in the hope that they, too, would be persuaded to do likewise. Now I told no one. It wasn't just that I wished to conceal that grotesque sense of depletion that so often accompanied my foraging into that kingdom of the old. I was also ashamed.

Miss Moberly's senescent congregation was seated in the vicinity of the tall windows through which the bright sun streamed. One or two old women knitted or talked or did both, but for the most part they sat silent, perhaps shaking from an infirmity such as Parkinson's disease, or hunched in one of the velvet green armchairs in a position which allowed them most relief from the problem of thin flesh over sharp bones. Many had canes by their chairs, several muttered quietly to themselves, one preferred to stand in her chromium walker, and another, wearing a pink cardigan and with an arcane srtip of metal across her head (which thus flattened her yellow-white hair) was stretched out on a sofa and gazed across at the tennis players clearly visible through the leafless trees over the street. There was one old man.

Miss Moberly began by leaving the 't' off my surname of Bryant and went on to describe me as primarily an author of children's books dealing with animals. It was at that juncture that I testily decided to change the story I was going to read them, from a ghost story set in Cornwall to a more somber one that dealt with sexual ambiguity and which had not the vaguest reference to pets nor vaguest appeal to a juvenile market.

Just as the Social Events Director concluded her erroneous remarks, the old lady in the pink cardigan screamed out angrily from her window seat. "Those kids are naked over there. Someone should call the police!"

One of the nurses crossed quickly to her, for the tempestuous grimalkin had grabbed her cane and was thudding angrily at the glass pane with its rubber ferrule.

"That's all right, Nelly. It's just the tennis players. It is much warmer out there than you might suspect. And then for hot-blooded youngsters — with all that activity . . ."

"It's just to spite us, I know what they're at. I've seen that little slut out there before."

"She's hardly naked, dear," the uniformed woman said soothingly.

But Nelly was not to be deflected so facilely from her protest. "Well *he* is! Look at that creature — flaunting his ugly body to upset all of us."

The interchange was brought to a halt by another diversion. I was turning to the first page of my short-story when the old man spoke up.

"I can't hear the speaker from here," he whined. He was sitting in proximity to the acerbic critic of the young tennis players.

"How do you know, Herb? He hasn't said anything yet!" The new voice belonged to a tall, birdlike woman sitting immediately in front of me. She seemed, at least from her features, to be full-witted and even smiled encouragingly at me from behind steel-framed spectacles.

"Herb is a bit of a complainer," she explained, in a firm voice quite loud enough for him to hear.

"Can I come and sit on the other side of you, Sir," he said in his high tremolo. "My best ear's that side, you see."

It occurred to me that I'd never get started at all if this interrupting continued. "Come on over, then," I said loudly — too loudly — "it'll be nice to have a bit of male back-up with all these lovely ladies around me."

That brought the expected titter from most of my audience but it was lost on the Grassmere inmate sitting opposite.

"You'll only start grumbling about your darned eyes if you do, Herb." Adding as she continued to look directly at me. "He's got a cataract problem. He's always moaning about the light. That's why we stuck him up near Beverely with his back to the window, isn't it Miss Moberly?"

But he was already tottering unsteadily in my direction, leaning heavily on his walking stick. I eyed him as he approached. One of the nurses immediately hurried from her seat to aid him in his erratic progress. He stuck out an elbow for her to support.

Herb, I noticed, was a little man, perhaps an octogenarian. His eyes were watery and weak under a close-cropped white head. He was cleanshaven although whoever had shaved him hadn't done too neat a job, judging by the patches of silvered whiskers about his cheekbones and chin. His neck was a wattle of red flesh and seemed hardly firm enough to support the rather large head. Below all that was even more of a mess — what with the foodstains down his rumpled shirt front and old grease patches shining from a virtually buttonless vest that he wore under a too large, brown jacket which looked itself like a Good Will reject. I had often noticed at other such geriatric institutions that the few old men they contained looked infinitely scruffier and frailer than their female counterparts. But Herb had a dishevelled quality all his own.

No sooner had he sat down on my right than the prophecy of the old girl facing me was vindicated.

"The light hurts me eyes a bit. I can't see you but perhaps I can hear if you speaks up. Most of 'em don't you know. That's why I don't usually come to these reading things."

"Shut up!" said another woman whom I hadn't noticed hitherto.

Miss Moberly recognized a newcomer slowly approaching on the arm of yet another white uniform. "This way, Agnes, he hasn't started yet. He's still talking to Herb."

I decided to change the situation then and there. They'd be bellyaching and interrupting for the rest of the afternoon if I didn't get things under way. "This story is from my book *LOVE & THE WAITING GAME,*" I began, and started to read my rather inappropriate tale in the confessional idiom, of a Cornish sex scandal on a farm which involved a middle-aged invert. The story was entitled "Cousin Petherick & The Will."

Halfway through my narrative Ms Pink Cardigan informed us all that she could now observe more nude tennis players and a hitherto silent member of my elderly audience announced that she, too, had visited Galiano Island where part of my story was located. But such minor interruptions were not unusual and after an encouraging smile and slight pause, I rammed fresh vigor into my voice and continued as if nothing had happened.

It was with the conclusion of the tale, with its grim revelation of a man's embarrassing affection for another that unusual things began to happen. They started with old Herb, when I had concluded with my standard invitation for questions or comments.

"Was — was that man — that Cousin Petherick — real?" he asked quietly.

The hag across from me glared through her thick glasses.

"He was disgusting, that's for sure!"

Herb ignored her and her displeasure.

"A farmer, you say. A farmer like me. More like me than you might all think. Only I was down there to California. Apple orchard we had in the Pajaro Valley, down there near Santa Cruz."

"Young man," said the hag, 'You seem clean-living and that. Why do you dredge up all that kind of filth, eh? Don't you ever spare a thought for the beautiful things of life?"

By now I was wishing that I had not succumbed to that fit of perversity and had read a different, more innocuous story. Not that I was ashamed of this one — or reluctant to account for my literary products. But I was hardly demonstrating courage or candour before these old things who had enough to do to hang onto life when at the clammy brink of death, than to wrestle with the problems of the sexually persecuted, the woes of those thrust by the vortex of procreation to the circumferences of life. Or so I thought. And so, seemingly, did Miss Moberly who was calling for general attention prior to thanking me and bidding me farewell. But not old Herb.

He wasn't holding up his shaking hand to protect his bleary eyes from the light any more. He was addressing his Grassmere sisters. "That — that man he was talking about? The fat one who made the will? That could've been me!"

"I didn't know you were *Cornish*, Herb," the advocate of Life's Beauties snapped. "In any case, you were a widower before you joined us here. You told me yourself. No children, I understood, but a widower nevertheless."

But he didn't seem to connect with her words. Either that or he was indifferent to them. "Mr. Bryan took me back long before that," he said slowly. "Long, long before Majorie and Vancouver. Down there to California it was. Off the old Aptos Road we had our place. Charley Parkhurst and me. We used to watch the trains go through to Santa Cruz. The Southern Pacific that was. We'd take the buggy over to Soquel and then on to Capitola in the cove. Jest Charley and me that was. Went swimming from the Ocean View Hotel in Aptos, too. We'd lie in the sun and listen to the sea lions — when there wasn't no fog, that is."

"Mr. Bryan doesn't want to hear your old stories, Herb," Miss Moberly remonstrated, a smile etched with the severity of the Mt. Rushmore carvings across the lower half of her powdered face.

"He's senile, that's what Herb is," contributed an unnamed other.

"We're all senile, aren't we Miss Moberly? Only we don't want to believe it." This time a tiny woman, almost hairless, piped from the very back row.

"Speak for yourself, Kitty," called out my witch adversary of the steel-rimmed glasses — without bothering to turn her head to recognize the voice's owner. "Anyway," she continued, "I want to ask Mr. Bryan about Devonshire cream. My husband, the late Mr. Arthur Weston, was from Torquay and always used to go on so about the clotted cream and how delicious it was."

I drew breath willingly; only too ready to switch the topic and *always* primed to give my mini-spiel on the subtle but major differences between English Devon and Celtic Cornwall. But my only peer of gender in the lounge of Grassmere Long Term Care Facility wasn't about to be deflected.

"Your man, that Cousin Petherick he never knew about himself, really, did he? I mean he put all that in his will about liking the other chap and leaving his money to him. But they didn't . . . they weren't . . ."

It wasn't just because of the pain of his faltering, but the sheer misery of the old man's appearance that firmed up my resolve. He was salivating freely now and his head rocked wild-ly — like one of these plastic caricatures of birds that keep dip-ping huge heads into empty tumblers — in the windows of some sleazy stores. "They weren't really lovers," I announced distinctly. "You're right, they were not exactly that."

"We were," Herb said to the burgeoning silence. "Charley and me was what you could call lovers. Out on the beach the first time. In public you might say."

"I don't see why we have to sit here and listen to unbridled filth" said the steel spectacles, sitting, if it were humanly possi-ble, even more upright. "Miss Moberly, where is my wheelchair? I've got to go you-know-where."

"Just one moment, Nora. Now before we all have our tea and cookies, I just want to say to Mr. Bryan —"

But like old Herb, I, too, was beyond niceties. "Why *now*?" I almost yelled at him. "Why do you have to tell all this *now*?"

He had to struggle with that — as if the problem was of such magnitude it would only yield to immense effort. If that awful head shook any more, I told myself, it was bound to fall off. It was only then I realized the old man was quite devoid of teeth. But quiver and shake, lick lips without managing to contain his drool, finding it terribly hard to shape words in that ever-shrinking palette — in spite of all such obstacles of his, he was determined to strive for the words which he had eluded or repressed for so long.

"That Petherick was a kind of virgin, weren't he? Not me. Charlie and I had it off. Not just the once but two times. But you see we never *talked* about it. And no one thought of will-making down there in California. But we should have spoken, I reckon. If I'd told him what I'm telling you then it would've all been different mebbe. Not all wasted like for that Petherick of yours and his Jimmy Tehiddy. There would have been no Marjorie, come to think of it. Fancy that! Not if the two of us had come clean about what we felt for each other when we had the apple orchard."

"I understand," I told him, although I really didn't.

"In any case," said Miss Moberly, now physically standing

between us so that we could only converse through the unrelenting white of her uniform.

"Tea-time is hardly the appropriate occasion for *that* kind of talk. Goodbye, Mr. Bryan, on behalf of all of us at Grassmere. And thank you so much for your odd little tale."

"My pleasure," I replied mechanically.

"Old Charley," said Herb, "fancy my remembering old Charley after all these years. Handsome one he was, you know. But proud! No one took no liberties with Charlie Parkhurst. Punch you in the teeth if you was to call him some name what he didn't like."

I stood up to go, squeezing past Miss Moberly for a final word with the old chap. "After that I should level with you," I said to him in a lowered voice. "I'm gay myself, of course. But for us it's easier than back when you were talking about. Anyway goodbye," I said holding out my hand.

He took it and we shook together, symbiotically, for a few seconds. He was patently summoning up a fresh spurt of words.

"Gay was you? Course it wasn't so happy a time then. It was all uphill work in the Twenties and the the Depression right after. Jesus, the work on that orchard was hard for just two guys what couldn't afford no help. No, I can't say we was gay exactly. But we had our fun and that. We made our own bed, you know. All the furniture in the shack, come to that. Then Charlie was some carpenter. And I was o.k. at the rough stuff."

"What — what happened to Charley, Herb?" I asked — really anxious to be on my way but wishing also to do the polite and kind thing. "Dunno," he said, for him quite sharply. "Dunno what happened. Probably married and settled down like me and Marge. He was originally from New Hampshire. May have made his way back there. Long dead and gone now, I expect."

Then Herb smiled broadly, revealing gums from which the pink had almost disappeared. "I sure got it all right in this place," he said. "What with just me and all the women falling over me — got it made I have!"

I gave his arm a nudge, and felt only bone. "It comes to us all," I told him with a jocularity that was absolutely false. Then I smiled inanely at my erstwhile audience of oldsters whose combined age covered centuries — before fleeing their patient presence for the easier deceptions of the tennis-court world outside.

# Bowen Island Confessions

It was three days before Ian McLean's sixty-second birthday, or so the architect told us as we sailed from a West Vancouver marina, heading for Bowen Island and a picnic on a sunny June day.

Ian, who was taking Ken and me while leaving his wife back at home immersed in the cultivation of her terraced garden, was someone the Irish like to describe as a 'beautiful man.' In his case that had nothing to do with looks for although he appeared considerably younger than his years, his face was scarred by long-departed acne and was wrinkled and chafed from hours of exposure to wind and sun from the time spent on the craft we were now sailing. His eyes were too close, also, to qualify him as handsome. No, Ian's beauty was a matter of the spirit, for I cannot remember meeting anyone more equable, more even of voice and more genuinely willing to give of himself in the cause of friendship. In short, a nice guy.

He and Lorraine were childless although their thirty-year-old marriage exuded a rich sense of harmony. I never recall him addressing her harshly and even on those rare occasions when he frowned or his mouth tightened, it seemed invariably in the cause of social justice or in displeasure at hurt or misfortune to a friend or acquaintance and never in emotional conflict with the words or actions of someone under his roof or sitting at his table.

So it was not unexpected, as the three of us sat in the warm sun in the scrupulously clean stern quarters of his four-berth sailboat, that we smiled or laughed to each gentle rise or fall of the swell out in the Gulf of Georgia and that my own spirits felt as buoyant as Sea Mist herself as she cut through the gray-green water, sending silver arcs of spray right up to the gunnels as we sped with the summer breeze.

"I do hope we're not taking you away from other things," Ken volunteered, for we had called up that morning after breakfast to enquire if an earlier promise for a sail was to be confirmed for that day.

"Certainly not!" our host exclaimed. "You know Lorraine would only have come if I had insisted. Sailing is far down her list of preferences. And I would not have gone on my own if you two chaps hadn't telephoned and reminded me of our arrangement. So really I owe you."

From then on we chatted mainly about sailing — which meant questions from us two landlubbers with Ian deftly avoiding the more arcane nautical jargon and explaining the ways of the sea in a language an intelligent child would have understood.

There was a brief period when our intercourse was interrupted by the dreadful chatter of a hovercraft on, presumably, some air-sea rescue business. Shortly after that our skipper brought out a six-pack from below as we turned south in order to view the lip of Stanley Park at Ferguson Point which looked like a tongue of green grass, with its gaily colored umbrellas shading the tables and chairs before the teahouse restaurant.

To the left of us the crowded fingers of the West End thrust up into the blue and further around the arc of our vision we could now see the Burrard and Granville bridges. And then the lower buildings of Kitsilano, where we lived, appeared; and the grey university towers as final ikons of human habitation on that stretch of Pacific coast, huddled on the promontory of Point Grey.

Neither Ken nor I had ever seen the city precisely from that perspective before. In the relaxed company of the native Ian and on the privacy of the Sea Mist, we were content to make commonplace noises of appreciation.

"God, it really is beautiful, isn't it?"

"We take far too much for granted living here. Then so much of the time we're on the inside looking out — and then you don't always realize the grace of Vancouver."

Ian swigged his Molson's and tended the tiller again. We both looked at him expectantly. Not that he'd been asked a question, but having both commented on the view it seemed somehow polite to attend his contribution. However, it appeared the vessel needed some special degree of maneuvering at that juncture for he looked only out to sea. The bow turned sharply westward and the odd shaped Vancouver Centennial Museum which looked rather like a bleached 'coolie's hat' was suddenly off our stern.

"That's Nanaimo due west," Ian announced. "Only we'll soon be turning to starboard and Bowen. Look out for the boom as we change about."

He was as good as his word, and there was scarcely time to duck under the swinging pole before we were describing a large semi-circle and eventually heading towards the hump of Bowen Island. A Nanaimo-bound ferry came up on our starboard beam and we all three waved back to the children clustered on the deck high above us. The next minute we were bobbing violently up and down in the ship's wake. I rather enjoyed that but glancing across at Ken I realized he was by no means as happy with the sudden undulation.

"We'll soon be in the lee of the harbor," Ian caught my look and told my room-mate, "Sorry about that."

As we approached our destination which was growing more distinct, Ian appeared ever more blissful.

"Gosh, I'm glad you boys reminded me about this outing of ours. Bowen is something special for me. For Lorraine, too." There was a tiny pause. "I don't know why we don't come over more often, really I don't."

Instead of elaborating on the topic he rather abruptly asked one of us to take the painter for landing and the other to slip the fenders over the sides of the craft.

It was not until the three of us — Sea Mist safely moored in the snug cove — were toiling up the hill away from the water, that he returned to the subject of Bowen and its attractions for the two of them. At first I thought that we were just strolling haphazardly until we chanced upon a suitable place to sit down and eat the contents of the wicker hamper Ken had packed and I was carrying, but suddenly Ian tugged at my arm and indicated a narrow path I was to take.

"Come on, I've just decided to share our favorite place with you fellows. I'll go ahead, though, as it gets a little rough at first."

"You used to come here a lot then? I hadn't realized," I told him.

"*Used* to is it. In the old days it was every weekend. But I'm talking about *aeons* ago!"

I smiled inwardly at his last words. As a Cornish Celt from a village dating its origins some fifteen centuries earlier, I felt rather like a Rothschild or a Rockefeller listening to the boasting of riches by a Penticton bank manager! But I respected Ian too much to even hint at a cultural sneer. In any case, he wasn't finished with reminiscence.

"It was up here that I proposed to Lorraine." His voice took on an even more plangent tone than usual. "It was a foxtrot we'd been dancing. To one of those gramophones you wound up?"

How like Ian to use 'gramophone' rather than 'phonograph,' I mused. But his mild version of Anglophilia didn't irritate me as did that of other native North Americans. It didn't reek of snobbishness and certainly was not expressed to ingratiate himself with me.

"It was a wonderfully warm June night and we both decided to slip outside for a breather. Oh, the stars! . . . the scent of roses! June, 1939 it was. Heh — you guys weren't even born!"

Ken quickly corrected him on *that* point, although laughingly admitting at our friend's insistence that we had both been little boys at the romantic moment he was describing.

By this time we had left the earlier track and found ourselves in a place that, I must say, I found enormously appealing. It was obvious that many years earlier, the path we were now on led through landscaped gardens of considerable extent and variety. Unpruned roses, their blooms now small but infinitely fragrant, covered disintegrating hedges, obscured fallen trellises, and ran rampant over dimly perceived lawns that had all but returned to more anarchic meadows.

And between the roses in their June extravagance we walked through other momentoes of a late, great, exercise in cultivation on these southern slopes of Bowen Island. There were giant clumps of delphinium and lupin in a variegated sea of blue and mauve, while splashes of snow-on-the-mountain, London Pride, magenta mesembryanthemum, and purple wigella indicated the prior presence of well-stocked rockeries.

Passing through this sea of color: radiant blemishes across the green land, we came eventually to the dissolving remnants of the large house from which had once emanated the intelligence which had ordered the acres of gardens. In part it was blackened by fire and charred beams poked ends through the healing foliage of the ubiquitous briars. Here Ian stopped and we gathered, one of us at either side of him.

"That was it," he said quietly. "That is the resort we young people used to visit at weekends when the world was sane."

"It's lovely," Ken murmured.

I was about to echo my room-mate's sentiments with something equally banal. (How is it we so often tend to clothe the breathtaking with the verbally mundane?) But I happened to note Ian's expression. By the look in his eyes I sensed he was no longer in accord with our positive mood — and that forestalled my contribution to words on that scent-laced air where quietness reigned in a measure of stillness that hushed our spirits.

"There was so much happiness here," Ian said quietly. "The Goddards, Freddy McBeath and his sister Helen. Chris Ward who'd bring his own sax and often join the band. Right over there, beyond those bushes were the tennis courts where we had such fun playing doubles."

I looked beyond the sumptuous blossoms of overgrown rhododendrons and could still make out a patch of meshing through the screen of morning glories which clung all over it. Whatever Ian was feeling, I could only respond with brimming spirits to the almost jungle riot of that westcoast garden now freed of the reins of man. But it was Ken who spoke and I was once more taken aback by the close approximation of the thoughts circling in his head to those abounding in mine.

"There's something magical about it all," he observed. "There's surely some Sleeping Beauty behind all those brambles and briars awaiting her prince. And apart from that, isn't there a fascinating melancholy about nature's repossession of things?"

By now we were walking through the charred remains of the resort-hotel; could see room after room of bared floors through which foliage had thrust up, and ivy and periwinkle snaked past shattered windows and climbed towards the visible sky. Even I was surprised by the vehemence of Ian's next words.

"No!" he said, with an anguish that trembled his voice. "It's dreadful what has happened. You don't see — neither of you understand. This was very precious to those of us who knew it in our youth. And now vandals have come and desecrated a sanctuary. Their filthy hands have brought their spray-cans. Look! Look at their ugly words and see what the arsonists have done to a place that was worth so much more than their runtish minds could ever appreciate!"

His outburst trailed off into the thickets of our silence. I pretended interest in a fluttering cabbage white butterfly over the wrecked verandah, profoundly conscious of how still the air was, there by the remnants of the resort; and that no birds sang.

"The hooliganism over the buildings — I can find no excuse for it, Ian," I told him. "But what happened to the gardens — you can't blame that on human ignorance, surely."

But our architect friend was suddenly in no mood for opposition.

"Yes, indeed, people are at fault. Strangers came, and with their eyes blind with dollar bills, bought the place, speculated, and finally saw just the acreage as profitable. Just like all over Vancouver. People have come and destroyed what they found. We had something *good* here, I tell you. Oh yes, you can sneer and say it was just a backwater of the British Empire and that we were stupid in 1939 when we were so proud to be both British and Canadian. But what we were and what this place stood for is something interlopers can never understand."

(And there was no doubt that the stress he placed on 'interlopers' was meant very much to include the two of us.)

Now Ken, although quieter spoken than I and infinitely calmer, is also dedicated to the notion of fairness — and obviously thought that Ian was being ingenuous.

"You're an architect yourself, Ian. You've made your own contribution to changing the face of Vancouver. And very positively at that, let me add." Maybe Ian didn't want to be placated. In any event, he continued in comparable vein. "None of you who come here can belong in the same way that those of us who grew up here do."

To say that I did not enjoy seeing our friend so hard in contrariness, would be to put it mildly indeed. But it was Ken who sought now most energetically to heal this rift which had surfaced so precipitately between us.

"Why don't you try and describe it to us, Ian?" he said placatingly.

"I've told you already. It's to do with a different generation and a world that's dead and gone." He made no attempt to conceal his bitterness. But Ken was Americanly persistent. "The Southern California I grew up in was all orange groves and is now mile upon mile of housing tracts. Yet if I took you there I'd try and make it real for you in the way it was for me as a child. Unless you simply insist we are unwanted trespassers and don't want us to understand."

I was relieved to see Ian smile, albeit wanly.

"I always over-react here. That's why Lorraine refuses to come back anymore. We did about five years ago and had a really big quarrel. She accused me of investing the joint with too much emotion because I said it was the only place I'd had experiences that weren't somehow marred. But that didn't impress Lorraine. She just refuses to 'hang onto the past' as she calls it."

"Will you please try and flesh it all out for us?" I asked, adding my petition to Ken's, for fear Ian had already forgotten it. "You could tell us about it while we have our picnic."

He looked from one of us to the other, trying, I think, to gauge our seriousness. I suppose we smiled or nodded encouragingly for he seemed to sag slightly as if in acceptance of our joined wish. "Let's move to the top of the headland," he suggested. "It's the best view and will help to jog my memory."

So it was, stretched out on a grassy bank, the derelict resort behind us as we faced out across Howe sound towards the concealed harbor of Horseshoe Bay, Ian McLean began to recall his youth in that place.

I can speak here of the galleon clouds riding in from the west under which gulls wheeled and cried; of the ridge of high cirrus, like candy floss stretched the length of the Coastal Range to the north of Vancouver, and of those cheerful smudges of disordered flowers in a garden run riot, where hummingbirds darted in staccato profusion, and where the heavy scent of roses sweetened the brine from the sea far below.

But Ian described another world. One which had lain in the gentle embrace of order: a time when seagulls dutifully followed ferry wakes to trim Victoria and sun-tanned Borneo Bishops dined formally in the sky at the staid Sylvia Hotel facing English Bay. It was a world where over vast horizons, the League of Nations died in the ashes of a defeated vision, and Stukka dive-bombers pounded Guernica — but that was far from the realm that Ian and Lorraine inhabited as the sandglass of the Thirties ran out.

"There was beautiful Margot McDermott, a singer who was engaged to Eric Svenholm whose hair and eyebrows were so blond they were almost white. He was killed in North Africa and Margot died of cancer on VJ Day. I remember precisely because my mother wrote to me and told me when I was in a Canadian Army Field Hospital near Arnheim and had just learned that I wasn't, after all, going to lose my left leg."

"The music?" I asked him gently. "What was the music you listened to here?"

"There were stone steps over there where that peony bush is. She would be all in white and trill away with the dance orchestra, all those lovely operatic notes from One Night of Love. But afterwards it wasn't Grace Moore she mentioned. She would cling to Eric's fingers as he spun her around on the granite dias below, and call out to us that she was our westcoast answer to Winnipeg's Deanna Durbin. That would always bring cheers, for Deanna Durbin was very popular with us. We'd all seen the latest movie she'd made. We would have been to at least one film the past week before coming over to dance on a Saturday evening."

"Did you discuss Adolf Hitler and believe in The Maginot Line?" Ken wondered aloud. "I gather the earth was blowing away in southern Alberta, just as it was in Oklahoma. There was a Dust Bowl shared as well as the Depression."

Ian shook his head. "Maybe we ought to have done, but we didn't. We were proud of The Granville Street Bridge which was still new and we wondered if King George and Queen Elizabeth would get as far west as us. We were fond of saying 'super' and thought the acme of modernity summed up in 'stream-lined.' We thought we had inherited the greatest century as well as the greatest empire the world had ever seen, and I knew that this splendid hotel and gardens was the closest I'd ever get to paradise."

Then without warning he suddenly laughed; brushed a faintly age-mottled hand against a bee-humming clump of blue geraniums.

"You are thinking of something funny that happened here in the gardens?" I asked.

But our friend shook his grey-curled head. "Not really. Just that apart from *God Save The King* and *Land of Hope And Glory*, both of which could easily bring tears to our eyes, the only other patriotic song we knew was *The Maple Leaf Forever* — certainly not *O Canada!* Oh, and also of how bloody different everything has turned out!"

That last sentiment seemed to agitate him so much that he could no longer sit still. We got to our feet, too, and followed a few paces behind as he climbed to the peak of the bluff where the mild breeze was stiffest and danced about the locks on the head of each of us. Up there on the ridge, he sat down again and stared for a while at the bright waters of the gulf. We sat down just below him. In spite of the zephyr it was pleasantly warm and as long as one faced seaward the sense of past cultivation was dimmer than anywhere we had so far traversed.

"You know, guys," Ian said suddenly, breaking his reflection. "You must think I'm some awful kind of rah-rah imperialist. And I'm *not*, you know."

We made mildly disclaiming noises, hoping he would continue with his recollections. Our grunts seemed to work.

"I told you about coming to this place with Lorraine and getting engaged, but I knew it long before then. When I was fourteen or fifteen I had a little skiff and unknown to my parents — who would've been horrified — I used to sail over here with a neighborhood friend. Right down there we hid a pile of pennies

— our secret treasure trove we called it. That spot was the only part of the place that wasn't landscaped in those days. It's odd. Now I stress the marvellous gardens but my friend and I much preferred it down there. I guess it was easier to hide in the long grass and there were no adults around to bother us."

"I had a place like that to hide in," I told him. "It was on our farm in Cornwall where I knew it was unlikely my father would come looking for me, and just far enough from the farmhouse for me to pretend I couldn't hear my mother if she hollered for some chore to be done. It was beyond an orchard and it was always cool and damp there in the marsh-meadows. I remember great clumps of yellow irises as well as bullrushes to hide from grown-ups."

"I guess all boys seek out places like that if it's at all possible," Ken added. "But for us in spreading suburbia down there in Southern California, it was often in the piles of building materials that we'd make a hiding place and spy on the grown-ups. To see but not be seen, means an awful lot to kids, I remember."

Ian looked into the middle distance. "I — I don't think what I'm talking about was quite the same," he said slowly. "No, now as I remember closely, I know that it was very, very different."

I fear I was on a totally contrary wavelength to Ian, at that moment. "You know, whenever I go back to Cornwall nowadays and see the revolting hardtop parking lots which have replaced cobbled courtyards and even the fields on the clifftops, I get so depressed I swear I'll never go back and see how the developers have ruined my birthplace."

"Well, I've really solved the problem," Ken said, grinning. "I never do go back to Covina any more."

But there was no response to our encouragement — at least not the kind of response that the general mood inspired by the view and the sunny day might have led us to expect. There was a further long silence from Ian. I tried to concentrate on a swift-flying cormorant skimming the surface of the sea, to relieve the growing tension.

"It was a total mistake," Ian came up with finally. "To have brought the two of you here was the dumbest thing I could've done."

"Nonsense!" Ken told him blithely. "Personally I consider it a privilege to be invited to share someone's past."

"I guess I could have managed if there'd only been *one* of you. Then I could have gone on lying to myself and Lorraine for the rest of my life.

But not now. Jesus, everything's all wrong now!"

"But Ian," I protested. "Just because a bunch of kids throw bricks through windows. And nature —"

But he was not minded to hear any of that again — from either of us.

"Oh, for Christ's sake! It's nothing to do with that! I've seen what a mess the place is in before now. And I couldn't care less about the fucking gardens!"

I'd never heard Ian cuss before, but it came now as dark froth on the torrent of his confession.

"Deep down, I suppose, I wanted the two of you here. Do you think you can plan whole expeditions without telling yourself what you're really doing?"

Only then did I realize how much Ian's strange mood was getting to Ken.

"Perhaps we'd better skip the picnic and head back to the mainland. We can take a rain-check, eh Ian?"

It occurred to me that the laugh Ken's suggestion evoked wasn't far from hysterical.

"A rain-check? On a day like this? You must be kidding!"

"It's you who doesn't seem to be enjoying the sun and the scenery," Ken pointed out.

"You're not hearing me," Ian said fiercely. "I'm talking about you — the *two* of you, understand?"

Ken and I exchanged meaningful glances. There were certain subjects that we had never broached with either of the McLeans — things we had assumed were common knowledge without needing articulation in the light of our affectionate relationship. For example, whenever the McLeans visited us they left their outdoor clothes on the bedspread in the *one* bedroom our house possesses. . . .

"I'm sorry if either of us has upset you," I began. "But I would've thought you knew us well enough to come straight to the point."

"Is it — is it something that's been bugging you for a long time?" Ken asked.

"No," was the reply. "I can't say that." Ian's voice was quite audible, even though I had the feeling at that point that he was no longer exclusively addressing us but rather having some weird kind of *colloquium* with himself.

"Lorraine has never shared this place with me. Not really. Then I've never given her anything but the surface of my life. Nor have I been honest about this resort all this time. I've never really loved that house, or the gardens. Only feared them . . . Ever since . . . ever since . . . Jesus! It's still hard to even mention that name. After what? Thirty years? Forty-three more like! Nor would I have ever felt the need to again if it weren't for these two with their bloody love for one another and all that united front stuff they put up. I could have had the same with Dennis, you know. We had it here all that lovely precious time — until that fucking war tore us apart. It would have been even better — Ian and Dennis — because I know we'd have remained faithful. Not all this phoney stuff . . . 'We both agree so much with what you say, Ian . . . We've been thinking this and that, Ian'. . . But that's just to hoodwink the likes of me. Oh, please don't join your voices ever again to tell me I'm still young, or any other nonsense. I'm just a lonely, unsatisfied old man, that's what I am. And the emptiness started in this damned place. It was here I started to run away from reality. And I've never stopped running until this day, just before my sixty-second birthday, for Chrissake! Until this very moment when I can say Dennis . . . Dennis . . . Dennis . . ."

I heard him sob the name yet again, and was glad that we were sitting below and could not see his face.

"A life of lies, how about that, eh? Dear old Ian. Calm and collected Ian . . . *Successful* Ian, they even say! And what the hell do any of *them* know about it? Lorraine, these two, Joe and Muriel, my sweet sister Jeannie — what do they know about a man who stopped living before he ever really started? Always — since that time here with Dennis — it's been like living the other side of plate glass. You smile — and she smiles back . . . You say she still has lovely hair and she tells you that you're still the laughing boy she met those years ago. But all the time you know something else — that the invisible glass is there and whenever you go to kiss or touch her, the cold of the glass is what hits your lips or your hands."

Then Ian sighed. I have rarely heard such a despairing hiss of air escaping from lungs. There was something horrible in the finality of it. But when he next spoke it was obvious that he

*187*

could no longer travel down that path he had so abruptly taken.

"I'm sorry," he said in altered voice, and now turning and looking down at us again. "What an exhibition I've been making of myself. Who would have thought one person capable of such floods of self-pity!"

"If — if there's anything you want to tell us," Ken prompted, "you know that we'd understand. And it would certainly never go beyond us."

But I could have told Ken he was wasting his breath. It wasn't just that awful sigh but the look I could now read in Ian's eyes. Because of some strange coincidence concerning the three of us and that place, he'd been forced to look back at something he simply found unbearable.

"Thanks," he muttered. "But there's really nothing to say. Not now. Not any more. It's all too late, you see. Look, let's try and forget my stupid outburst, will you? I reckon we should start on that picnic lunch, chaps. I think I could handle one of those chicken sandwiches you mentioned, Ken."

In the event, though, when we had unpacked everything and spread out the food on the mohair throw rug, I noticed he took nothing — except a glass of white wine. But if the picnic proved a somewhat disconsolate business, it was nothing compared to the voyage back across the water, which we did, by unspoken assent, right after we had replaced most of the food in the hamper.

The man holding tightly to the tiller in the stern was no longer the relaxed and amiable Ian of the journey out. He kept looking straight ahead all the time but it was hard to make out what his eyes were concentrating on. And his mouth stayed tightly clamped until we were again on dry land.

There at the marina, we made our stilted goodbyes by our respective two cars. In flat tones he asked us back to the nearby house but it hardly took genius to perceive the invitation was the most formal of gestures. And in any case, neither of us were minded to be present when this depleted Ian was again in the presence of the astute Lorraine.

So we returned to the city, to our little house in Kitsilano. Later that evening Ken called the McLeans to thank Ian for the outing. He didn't take long and when he came into my study he was wearing a perplexed expression.

"That was Lorraine I talked to," he said. "Ian hasn't come home. She thought he was still over on Bowen with us."

"What about the boat?" I asked. "Did she go down to the marina to meet us?"

"That was the other funny thing," Ken said slowly. "Yes she did and Sea Mist wasn't there. He must have taken off again."

That was over a month ago. Ian has still not returned home.

•